Let Me Marry You

Karen Tucci

True Heart Romance

Contents

Karen's Other Books:

Stand Alone Books:

<u>When the Dust Settles: A Sweet Romance with a Navy SEAL</u>

G & G Security Series (Coming 2025)
(The characters from When the Dust Settles cross-over in this series)
Operation: Heal my SEAL Book 1
Operation: Find my SEAL Book 2
Operation: Keep my SEAL Book 3
Operation: Train my SEAL Book 4

Second Chance Series:
<u>Starting Over</u>
<u>Moving On</u>

Big L' Ranch Series
<u>The Perfect Kiss: Book 1</u>

<u>The Perfect: Cowboy Book 2</u>
<u>The Perfect Match Book 3</u>
<u>The Perfect Christmas (Holiday Novella)</u>
<u>The Perfect Sheriff Book 5</u>

Best Friends Series
<u>Let Me Carry You</u>
<u>Let Me Marry You</u>

YA Cumberland Christian Prep School Series
The Big Score (Coming 2025)

Chapter 1

♥

HAWAII – THREE MONTHS AGO

Anxiety was a killer. It shortened Joe's breath and tightened his chest. Sweat speckled his brow despite the air-conditioned room. This wasn't part of the vacation plan.

Relax, he coached himself as he stared into the mirror, preparing himself for seeing Donna. Having a serious conversation with her about their future was proving more difficult than he had initially thought. How hard could it be to say, "Donna, let's keep dating?"

It was nearly impossible. With his dad sending him an onslaught of texts, nagging him about working for the company, Joe wanted to punch the practice mirror.

His phone vibrated again. Joe wiped his palm down his face, something he always did when nervous or frustrated — right now, he was both.

Stop ignoring your responsibility to this family.

Besides, you'll never make as much money at that park as you would with me.

> Your mother and I paid for your education. Not for you to waste away at some theme park.

After he read the first two texts that came through, he chuckled — a better choice than actually punching something he'd have to replace later.

"That *theme park* is my job, Geesh!"

> Your office is waiting for you. I expect you to fill it once you return from gallivanting on a tropical island.

> Don't let that girlfriend of yours sway your mind, either. You can have any woman you want. Don't limit yourself.

"Now he says I can get any woman I want. Whatever."

In school, he struck out. Every. Single. Time. As a tall, lanky, acne-ridden kid, girls ignored him until they needed to pass a test or complete a difficult assignment. Fast-forward fifteen years, and here he was with a six-pack, muscular arms, and a clear, smooth complexion.

On more than one occasion, he'd caught Donna ogling his bare chest. That part was great, but it wasn't about having other women. Joe didn't want to work for his dad. He was happy owning the business with Brent. Nor did he want a woman who didn't impact his decisions; wasn't that true love? Give and take on each other's part? That's what his mom told him, and he trusted her completely.

Within minutes he received a text from her. She always chose her words carefully when texting, but she and Joe had had many private conversations.

> Hi Dear. I hope Hawaii is just as beautiful as ever. When you get home from your vacation, how about you and Donna come over for dinner? Love and miss you. Mom.

The barrier Joe had been building between his father and himself was getting thicker and thicker. Blocking his father was a solution quickly approaching. He even stooped so low as to involve Joe's mom, always claiming that she needed to back him.

Joe read between her lines. *Dad wants to see you so he can harass you even more about working for him and make sure Donna isn't corrupting me.*

> We'll see, Mom. Love you. Talk soon.

Twenty minutes later, dressed and ready to escort Donna to the final activity Brent planned, Joe sent up a quick prayer. *Lord, thank you for the strength to branch out on my own. Please change my dad's mindset and heart, or give me the strength to end all ties with him. Please watch out for Mom. In Jesus' name, Amen.*

"Wow!" Joe exclaimed the moment Donna opened her door. The thigh-length, spaghetti-strap summer dress lay perfectly on her hips and flowed out. "You look beautiful."

"Thank you." She blushed.

Donna's blonde ponytail cascaded over her shoulder in one tightly wound curl. Whenever she was nervous, she twirled her ponytail tightly around her finger, repeatedly. By the time she stopped, she produced a tightly formed curl like the one Joe saw now.

"Everything okay?"

She offered a semi-convincing smile. "Yup, Got my bag; let's go."

Joe brushed aside his insecurity and held out his elbow as Donna wove her arm through. If it was the last thing he did, Joe would show his father that his and Brent's business would bring him more money than he could spend in twenty lifetimes, and he would get his girl. The only question remaining was if that girl was Donna or not.

"I say we don't break up." Joe's tone was not what he'd planned. *Darn.* It sounded rehearsed and heartless - the exact opposite of what Joe thought he had perfected when practicing this speech in front of the mirror earlier this morning. Joe's fingers itched to pick one of the red hibiscus flowers lining the path he and Donna traveled. The timing needed to be perfect. He'd pluck one from the ground and gently place it behind her ear, and she'd agree that she enjoyed being with him as much as he did her.

He would finally get his chance to prove to this father and everyone else who rejected him that he was worthy and successful.

"No?" Donna's heart skipped. The trade winds controlled the eighty-degree temperature. Did the sweat forming at her hairline mean she was just as nervous as him?

Sadly, he'd started to believe the girls from his past — that something was wrong with him, you know, on the inside.

His confidence was fasting fast, even though his physical appearance seemed much improved.

He hadn't come to this conclusion on his own. Nowadays, with women giving him second glances and lingering looks, he assumed he must be relatively attractive, or they wouldn't look, right?

It was now or never. He just had to convince Donna that he could be a good boyfriend or at least give him a chance to show her that he could. He had this.

Certainty raced through his veins. He didn't want just any woman. He wanted Donna. Her laugh did crazy things to his stomach, so he acted silly just to hear her. Her soft skin and equally soft hair set him ablaze when they connected. Desire swam in the depths of her sea-green eyes — another sign in his favor — overwhelming him every time she looked at him.

Gently grasping her elbow, he tugged her to a stop. "Instead of making it a big deal, telling them we set this whole thing up, faking our relationship so they would develop theirs, I think we should just let this dissolve." He felt his jaw slack.

Wait, what did I say? That was definitely not what I practiced. His stomach churned. Where'd his practice words go? *Donna, I know you only agreed to pretend to date me, but I really like you. Could we see where this leads for real?*

He'd enjoyed spending time with her the last few months, building his courage around her. He never questioned it when it came to holding her hand, pulling her close, and even kissing her cheek.

He'd been pretending. *Liar,* his inner voice slapped him.

Who was he kidding? It had never been fake for him. He'd been attracted to Donna from the moment he laid eyes on her. He only suggested fake dating in case she laughed at him. Fortunately for him, she hadn't.

"Don't let fear rule you," Brent's words rushed through his head.

Joe never feared anything . . . except rejection.

Doubt twisted in his gut as he swiped his palm over his face. Locking eyes with her, he spoke with a nonchalance he definitely wasn't feeling. "Well, it looks like I'm a dollar bill and single again."

Phew. His cheesy line made her smile.

"If that's what you think is best," Donna retorted, crossing one arm over her midsection while twisting her ponytail with her finger. Joe knew that wasn't a good sign, but as his face raked over his surroundings, he saw Brent and Andrea waiting for them.

Joe stuffed his hands in his pockets. *Maybe what I practiced saying was what I wanted to say. Maybe what I said was what God wanted me to say.* He'd known from the beginning that Donna wasn't adventurous. He couldn't have a relationship with someone like that, could he?

Chapter 2

♥

Hawaii – Three Months Ago

Donna's heart plummeted, and her jaw started to drop, but she caught it at the last second. *How could I have been so dumb?* For her entire life, Donna had let someone else's situation dictate her decisions — big ones. She didn't have a choice with her dad, but couldn't she do something about this *thing* with Joe?

Look at that ocean, those palm trees, and the state flower growing wild. Paradise surrounded her. She reaped the trip as a reward by taking the full-time accountant and social media manager position Brent and Joe offered her.

Some reward, she silently scoffed.

Her feelings for Joe blossomed quickly after they made their agreement. Given the days and nights they spent together plotting and scheming, this shouldn't have surprised her.

Now, her heart had fallen deeper and deeper for the fun-loving, adventure-seeking hunk, Joseph Hudson Hartley.

Between the sweet scent of the hibiscus and the light splash of the Pacific Ocean on her skin, Donna heard Joe's first words — sweet and melodious — like a singing Zebra Dove calling out to her. Then, all too suddenly, Bang! Someone shot that bird out of the sky. She was that bird lying with both wings injured, knowing she was going to be alone . . . again.

Donna had never been great at reading the male species, but she'd thought they had chemistry. Granted, Joe's stunning good looks drew her in first. His chiseled jawline and muscular frame were hard to resist. His smooth face needed a more rugged appeal to match his body, but that wasn't a deal breaker. Her fingers longed to run through his perfectly messy hair — it fit his laid-back personality to a tee.

His smile faded. Then it reappeared, reminding her that this man could act, so she didn't know what he was thinking.

The once acceptable plan now showed its true colors — a colossal mistake! Probably the worst mistake she'd ever made. Her heart got tangled along the way with Joe's sweet words and gestures. She'd repeatedly told herself it wasn't real. Too bad her heart betrayed her, going rogue and falling for the man who had just broken things off with her. . . in Hawaii. Who does that?

The path they traveled ended. How fitting. *Did he plan that?* They reached Brent and Andrea, who were waiting for them on the sand. "Are you ready for this last excursion?" Brent asked, not hiding his eagerness.

NO! I am ready to hang glide without the hang glider. Breathe, Donna reminded herself.

She looked around at the excited faces, waiting for her to answer. Her stomach soured. Despair ran through her veins. The unknown adventure awaiting her, potentially leading to her early demise, wreaked havoc with her insides.

"Come on, Schweetheart," Joe used his best Bogart impression, "This will be fun."

Doubtful.

Brent smiled. "Listen to your man. It'll be a rush."

My man? If only!

Joe flashed his million-dollar smile, weakening her resolve.

Knowing it would be her last adventure with him, Donna mustered all the courage she could. "Okay, I'm ready."

Given Brent's look, she knew he had planned something intense for their final adventure. She hadn't expected anything less since extreme sports were born, bred, and cultivated in Hawaii.

Donna's heart thumped so loudly, she thought her friends could hear it for sure.

Joe gently grabbed her arm before she could step away. Her breath hitched. He leaned into her shoulder, his solid chest firing every nerve ending in her arm. If that weren't bad enough, the manly smell of wood and musk flooded her senses.

Without letting go, he wrapped an arm around her waist and gently brushed his lips against her ear. "Don't worry.

I know Brent. Anything he's planned will be safe and fun," he whispered, sending shivers down her spine.

Just one more. You can play this up so no one gets hurt. Well, no one except me. She'd unintentionally given her heart to Joe; he didn't ask for it. He didn't love her. She would disappear from his life just like Groot turning to dust in Rocket's arms in Infinity Wars, a movie she and Joe watched together one night in an attempt to make their relationship look more legitimate.

Brent tried to assure Donna that she was safe. "I've chosen an activity that requires a professional with us at all times." His look told her she wouldn't like this. . . at all.

"Skydiving! We're going tandem skydiving with Sky Hawaii!"

The heck I am! Donna's heart raced, and her stomach fell. Her knees buckled, and Joe instantly tightened his grip. "I can't do that," she spat out.

Andrea clapped her hands excitedly, but her smile faded when she shared a sympathetic look with Donna.

Hadn't she been selfless enough? She didn't need more guilt.

Andrea is engaged to Brent, and Joe gets to forget I ever existed. *What do I get out of this? A broken heart.* They should let her quietly bow out of this excursion — like that would ever happen.

"Tandem is much safer because the professional skydiver is strapped to the back of the jumper," Andrea said, attempting to convince Donna that she'd be okay.

Donna rolled her eyes. They all knew she hated heights. Why did people feel that over-explaining something would change her mind? Probably because it had in the past. It hadn't been that long ago that she screamed like a banshee when she zip-lined with Andrea despite her initial reservations.

That was the day she met Joe — the day her soul took flight.

Donna's mom always taught her to take responsibility for her actions, so she refrained from blaming Joe for being easy to fall for.

"Joe, you'll be the only one who can convince her." Andrea captured Brent's eyes and jerked her head to the side. "We'll be waiting in the car. I hope you come with us, Donna. It won't be the same without you."

Once Andrea and Brent were out of earshot, Donna stepped back. "Please don't make me do this," she said, crossing her arms over her chest. "I have done everything you three have asked of me. In the last five months, I've thrown up more than I have in my entire twenty-eight years on this planet."

Joe chuckled. "You're so dramatic."

"Not really, just reporting the facts." Donna deadpanned.

"Skydiving in Hawaii is. . ." He moved closer, and Donna's heart leaped. His hand cupped her elbow, then slowly caressed down her forearm until he laced their fingers together. "The pressure from free falling feels like the best hug you could imagine — a warm press against the skin that you'll instantly miss once you land." His eyes held hers, increasing her heartbeat — the only indication of life — even more.

Joe wasn't playing fair. His soft touch heated her skin. Did it mean anything that no one was around, yet he touched her with ease?

The trade winds sent his musky smell straight through her, pulling her closer to him like a magnet. His low, husky voice wore her down.

"What do you say?" Joe urged.

His pleading look caused her two-faced heart to melt.

None of this mattered. Once she got home, Donna had other things to focus on, so she could handle one last hoorah with Joe.

"I'm all in." The words plunged out of Donna's mouth. They sounded like a life-long commitment but felt like imminent death.

"Thank you." Joe wrapped his arms around her waist and pressed his chest against her. His heart beat erratically, competing with hers for first place. Not possible. Donna's fingers roamed over his strong shoulders, amazed by his upper body strength.

She hated how a few sweet words and one unforgettable hug had her jumping out of a plane! Why hadn't Donna focused on him dumping her? That might have prevented her from acting like she had a death wish.

As the plane ascended, Donna stared out the minuscule window. She couldn't control her jittery legs. *Am I having a heart attack?* Donna rubbed her palm over the center of her chest.

Joe placed his hand on her shoulder. She jumped, forcing him to step back and lift his hands in surrender.

"Are you okay?" he yelled over the plane's noise.

Donna shrugged and simultaneously shook her head.

He sat down beside her, gently turning her face toward him, removing her attention from the disappearing green grass below. "You've got this," he said, reaching for her hand, but she pulled away quickly. He raised his eyebrows in question.

"Sweaty." Talking was challenging. She heard her heart thump in her ears, her chest rising and falling faster the higher the plane ascended.

It'd only been ten minutes before she asked, "How high are we?"

Marc, the professional jumper assigned to her, studied a gadget on his wrist, "Just hit seven thousand."

"This is only halfway!?" Donna panicked.

"Unless you want to become one with the ground," Marc laughed.

"Seriously, Man?" Joe grabbed Donna's hand and squeezed it.

"You'll be okay. I'll meet you on the ground." Joe glared at Marc as he walked by him.

Aw. His protectiveness set her stomach into a fiery somersault. Too bad his words couldn't squash her fears.

Brent held the highest skydiving license, so he and Andrea would jump together. They looked like two kids in a candy store as they readied to hurl themselves out of the plane. Joe, one license below Brent, couldn't be Donna's tandem partner but could solo jump.

She lifted another prayer as Marc motioned her toward him.

Dear Lord, please let my mom know that I love her. Don't let her hold this over Andrea, Joe, or Brent. I could have said no. Please protect me if it's your will. She paused for a moment. *If I'm going to have broken bones or worse, please just bring me to you. Amen.*

What seemed like seconds later, Donna was hooked to a professional jumper. "Time to put on your goggles," he instructed.

Donna could only nod her head while she got them situated. Her stomach felt queasy. As she watched Brent propel him and Andrea into the sky, more prayers filled her mind.

"See you down there," Joe hollered back before he stuck his arms out wide and fell from the back of the plane, hooting and hollering.

"Remember," the professional barked in her ear, "we're only freefalling for sixty seconds. Then I'll open the chute."

Please help me through this, Lord. I can do anything for one minute.

Her feet, cement blocks, shuffled along as her expert pushed her along. She'd instructed, "Just jump no matter my pleas."

"Here we go." The instructor's weight pushed Donna from the plane.

Her stomach dropped immediately. "AHHH! Why did I do this this?"

She remembered — one last adventure with Joe. Tears pricked her eyes. She would have blamed the wind, but the goggles were protecting her. This seemed fitting. She'd let herself freefall for Joe and look where that got her. Hopefully, she didn't experience the same fate as her heart.

How long was a minute? Donna knew the obvious answer, but it seemed like she'd been falling for an eternity. Pull the chute already.

Donna's body jerked upward as if he heard her thoughts; her feet dangled down.

"What a rush, huh? Enjoy the view for the next few minutes," Marc encouraged.

It was beautiful.

After Donna landed from her fourteen thousand–foot jump, she threw up not once or twice but three times. Marc, previously strapped to Donna's back, escaped a disgusting fate by mere seconds. Despite her body's reaction, Donna proclaimed she had fun.

Joe handed Donna two towels — one wet and one dry.

"Thank you."

Once cleaned up, Donna spotted Joe looking uncomfortable. She noticed his hesitation before he turned back to face her. "Are you doing okay?"

"Not really. There's no way I'll ever eat again." The hollow feeling in her stomach ached.

He grinned. "I meant, are you okay with what we talked about?"

Donna wrapped her arms around her middle. "This was the plan. We did what we set out to do - Brent and Andrea gave each other a chance, fell in love, and now are engaged. So, like you said, our time is over." Did he notice her disdained tone? Probably. Did she care? No. Maybe.

If Joe realized she hadn't answered the question, he said nothing. What did her feelings matter anyway? They'd done what they set out to do — her brain knew that. Now, someone had to convince her very shattered heart that she and Joe were over.

Chapter 3

MARCH WAS A TRICKY month in New England. The snow melted relatively quickly, with temps in the high forties and fifties. Just when people had had enough of looking at their boots and ski pants, they stored them in the basement. Then, Wham! An early spring storm dropped six to eight inches of snow mixed with sleet and freezing rain.

That's what happened over the weekend. However, it didn't stop Joe from enjoying all his favorites: skiing, snow-boarding, cross-country skiing, snowshoeing, hiking, and mountain climbing. Now, he'd be golden if he could achieve a little success with his two other big problems: Donna and his dad.

Joe's phone rang through his truck's speaker on his way to work. He sighed, seeing his dad's name sprawled across the screen. "Come on, it's too early for this."

"Hello, Dad." Joe couldn't help his flat tone.

"I've got a great opportunity for you."

Joe shook his head and rolled his eyes.

"You listening?"

"Yup."

"Daniel finally retired. This is your opportunity to step into a high-level position without people claiming nepotism."

Joe dragged his palm over his face.

"It's time you give up your fantasy of becoming rich at that theme park of yours. You can sell your shares and invest in our business."

Joe wasn't the one who wanted to get rich. He wanted to have fun while working but couldn't explain that again.

"Not going to happen. You have no interest in me as a partner. You want to use me to your advantage so you can get rich." Joe's heart rate spiked.

"Why are you so stubborn? Your skills are necessary here at the family business."

"Why are you so blind? Brent and I are doing exceptional, and next quarter seems on target to exceed our last two quarters combined," content filled Joe's heart.

"Everyone has a great fourth quarter with Christmas sales. What about the rest of the year?"

"Brent and I have investor meetings coming up. Our business will make us millions, not that he or I care about money like you do."

"First of all, I don't see it that way. If you and Brent can't make it on your own, you shouldn't be in business. Besides, do you have the ability to run the business and work with investors? You are an engineer."

Joe hated how insecure his father made him feel.

"If you were willing to open your eyes, you'd see how prosperous our business will be. I have to go." Joe hung up without giving his dad a chance to respond.

One quick smash of his palm against the steering wheel gave him a sliver of release. What would it take for his dad to give up his dream of Joe joining the family business? The familiar looming darkness he felt when dealing with his dad was starting to settle in.

Lord, please shine your light over me. Clear my mind of all things dark. Help me to see you and your goodness.

Pulling into the parking lot, he blew out a hard breath, pushing his father from his mind.

He hadn't expected to see Donna and Brent's vehicles in the parking lot. *How early do these people get here?*

Strike one for any headway with his dad. Hopefully, he could win Donna over with a muffin from her favorite bakery. It was a shameful ploy to get back into her good graces after botching their relationship.

The songbirds greeted him as he exited his truck with the muffin bag in hand, pulling him back to the present. *Thank you, Lord, for the beautiful birds.* Joe could fix this, God willing.

The bell above the door chimed when Joe grabbed the handle and whipped it open. He caught her eye. Donna stood there with full-length black running pants and an oversized sweatshirt, stopping about mid-thigh, which is exactly where his gaze stopped.

Don't look there. Find her eyes. The last thing Joe wanted was for Donna to think he was checking her. Let's face it, he was. But besides being a red-blooded male, he was also a gentleman.

The heat that flooded him reminded him of the first time he'd felt that way with her. Donna had just finished her first time on a zipline. She'd rolled off the landing mat and sprawled out like a starfish. She grazed his abs as he caught her head before she smashed it on the ground, declaring she would never do that again.

"Thank you." Brent held out his hand toward the bakery bag. "Sorry, not sorry. This is for Donna."

Her eyes widened, and she pointed to herself as if to ask *me?*

"Don't look so surprised. If your man doesn't surprise you every once in a while like that, he's probably not the man for you," Brent stated nonchalantly.

"You sound like Andrea." Donna teased.

"What can I say? She makes a lot of sense," Brent shrugged.

Joe handed her the bag. He wanted to give her a greeting kiss on the cheek, too, but wasn't sure how she'd respond.

"Thank you."

He leaned in and softly spoke. "If you keep looking shocked that I did something nice for you, Brent might question our relationship." She smelled like lilacs, making him wish he was a bumblebee. Then he could hover around her all day.

He rocked back on his heels, feeling slightly uncomfortable with Brent staring at him. Since they'd returned from Hawaii, the two couples had continued to hang out, but he and Donna hadn't spent any time alone — understandably, since he butchered his well-rehearsed speech.

Joe had lost all the nerve after their tropical vacation. He probably could have moved on and explained things to Donna, but the nagging texts he'd been getting from his dad reminded him of his failure. 'Mom wants you over for dinner. Bring that girl. Unless you've messed that up already, too.'

He'd become the master at ignoring his dad's comments, but this one rang true. He had screwed things up, and admitting that to his old man was the last thing he'd do.

Her sea-green eyes captured his briefly until her full lips pulled his attention away. Was it possible that his attraction had grown even more for Donna?

Like metal clippings to a magnet, he was drawn to her — she was his north. He could always find his way with her by his side.

"Hey, Donna, did you hear about the nation's longest and fastest zip line? It runs across three states. Andrea checked it out and wants us all—"

"—Count me out." Donna interrupted. If the ones here had me screaming like someone was murdering me, could you imagine. . . I'd die on that thing."

Both men tried to hide a chuckle.

"Babe, you've been skydiving; you can handle a zip line," Joe encouraged her.

Her eyes spoke clearly — BACK OFF!

He hadn't meant to upset her but wanted more time with her. Another adventure like that would be perfect.

"When are we going?"

He heard Donna huff but ignored it, hoping she'd change her mind if he could talk to her alone.

"Tomorrow. That way, it won't interfere with our prep work and scheduling for opening day, but it requires a bit of planning, which we all know Andrea is all over. "

"Sounds like a blast."

"Sounds like I need a barf bag."

Joe laughed and then felt terrible. "I'm sorry. I thought you were trying to be funny."

"Don't worry, Donna. You can slow yourself down. It's a two-hour line, so Imagine you'll get comfortable quickly."

"Two hours?!" Donna shrieked.

Without thinking, Joe gently caressed her forearm and whispered. "This could be fun together." Her pulse point ramped up. Did she like the idea of spending time with him? Not that they'd be on the line together, but the drive there would be nice. Who was he kidding? He'd welcome a drive to the grocery store with Donna.

He studied Donna's expression, which flashed with concern.

Brent looked at them suspiciously. "Something is off with you two."

Donna gasped in his ear when he wrapped his arms around her waist and nuzzled his head into her neck. She stumbled backward as he led her toward the office. Hopefully, this looked playful and believable.

Once inside her office, Joe shut the door with his foot and released her.

"What was that?" Donna questioned, setting the bag containing her muffin on her desk. Her flushed cheeks made her even more beautiful.

"Sorry, Brent's suspicion made me nervous."

Donna ran her hands over the front of her shirt, smoothing out the "Joe wrinkles."

"Will you go with us?" Joe reached for her arm but pulled back, wondering if that would be too much.

She noticed. Her eyes dropped, watching him reel himself back. Was that a look of disappointment?

"Joe," she sighed, resting her arms on her hips. "No matter how much I want to spend time with you, I can't do that zip line." Donna turned, rushing to her desk.

What did she say? *Does she want to spend time with me?* Joe's heart high-fived his ribs.

Joe moved within an inch of her back, and the urge to wrap his arms around her overwhelmed him. Instead, he stuffed his hands in his pockets. "Please come with us."

"What happened to us dissolving the relationship? Your words, not mine." Her voice, meek and soft, riddled with hurt. Joe hated himself for hurting her.

"It was a mistake. I—"

Her office door flew open, causing Donna and Joe whiplash. Brent declared, "We are all set for tomorrow."

"Are you coming with us?" Joe's voice and eyes pleaded.

Her gorgeous green eyes bounced between Brent and him.

He wondered if a relationship could be enough for either of them. Would he ever get sick of trying to convince this non-adventurous woman to try some of his favorite pastimes? Would she get sick of him asking? Would she ever want him to stop?

The corner of her lip turned up. "Okay. I'll try it."

"Why did I agree to another thing that could take my life?" Donna's shrill urged Joe to grab her hand as they proceeded up the chair lift.

"This is why I don't ski." Donna looked over the side of the chair.

"Look right here." Joe gently turned her head toward him. He locked his eyes on hers, a dangerous move for him.

But if it helped her, he'd take a few flip-flops in his low belly.

Joe thought the quad chair was perfect since it would come to a stop for Andrea. Though she'd made significant progress walking again since getting her spinal implants after suffering from paraplegia in the same accident that had killed her parents, fast, quick movements, like hopping off a chair lift, are too risky.

He put his arm around her shoulders and turned her slightly to focus on him. "You'll be safe," he said.

"In your arms, maybe. Too bad we weren't on the ground, though."

Joe watched the pulse in her neck race faster than they were about to soar down the zip line. Did she mean the words coming out of her mouth, or was her adrenaline and anxiety talking?

Anticipation darted through his veins, hoping that her feelings were real

When they reached the platform, the crewman stopped the lift for Andrea. The guys lifted the bar, and Brent helped Andrea get out of the chair. Donna's right hand sported white knuckles on the sidebar.

"Come on, Sweetheart. Let's go. We'll have fun," he whispered in her ear.

She reluctantly let go just as Joe lifted her by the waist.

Securing the harnesses and watching the safety video only took thirty minutes. These men didn't care that Joe and Brent owned their own zip-line park or that Joe was the engineer for some of the lines; they still had to view the video.

The four friends were secured to their lines.

"The loser pays for dinner," Brent hollered.

"Not going to happen, Brent," Donna retorted. "The winner buys dinner. I'll be glued to my break, so I know it won't be me."

The layout impressed Joe. Four parallel zip lines, making racing friends a thrill. He was currently working on plans for the steepest zip line in America. Maybe that would impress his father. Probably not. Oh well.

"Ready?" The safety instructor hollered.

"No," Donna responded.

"Don't listen to her. We're ready," Andrea informed him.

"Gee, thanks."

"Set. Go!"

Joe waited a second, worried that Donna wouldn't go, but she did. His smile reached his ears. He couldn't deny it; this woman had a hold of him.

Chapter 4

WHEN WOULD DONNA STOP letting people dictate her decisions? There was crazy, and then there was this! What had Donna been thinking? She hadn't been; she just leaped when the instructor said go. So far, she hadn't screamed like Freddy Kruger was following her either — a definite win since the first time she'd zip-lined.

Despite her sheer panic and distress that day, she'd met Joe, making it all right. If they were actually dating, that old saying *and the rest was history*, would apply. Unfortunately, for her, *she* was history.

Although they were continuing to see each other since they'd arrived home, which she hadn't been expecting, he had become more physically distant.

If she were being honest, Donna missed how he'd grab her hand or pull her in for a side hug. She loved the kisses on the forehead — not as good as the temple, but he'd been inching his way closer.

Now, he spent most of his time stumbling over his words again, which didn't make sense to her since he had been the one to state that things needed to change.

Joe slowed when he reached her. "You doing okay?"

Not really. "Yes, enjoy the ride. I'll see you at the next platform."

And he was gone. Her spirits dropped. She shouldn't let that bother her. If she wanted him to stay, she should have said that. All Donna's life, she'd tried to make everyone around her happy. Was she a people pleaser? Not exactly. She figured that if she made people around her happy, they wouldn't leave her. Turns out that she's either horrible at making people happy, or people just suck. The jury was still out.

According to the safety instructor at the platform, Donna had only been about five minutes behind the others. Donna felt bad. She told them they didn't have to wait, but actually, they did — company policy.

"How do you feel?" Joe dragged his clip along the safety line until he was directly in front of her.

"Good."

She looked down, but he gently lifted her chin with his finger, their eyes connecting. "To stay that way, you should avoid looking down," he chuckled and winked.

This instructor reviewed the safety procedures with them. Joe squeezed Donna's hand, and her arm lit up. She needed to control these reactions but had yet to figure out how. He caressed her arms this time, and warmth ran through her upper body.

Oh goodness, then he leaned in and whispered, "You sure you're good?" Why did he have to be so protective? Is there anything more sexy than a caring, sweet man who's also protective? Nope!

Her throat felt like sludge, so she nodded.

The instructor counted them down again, and they were off. Joe didn't wait, and Donna didn't use the hand break. . . as much, so she kept up with the others better, only arriving at the last platform about a minute after her friends.

The weather started to turn on the last stretch of the line. Since it was the longest, the instructors sent them on their way with a quick safety reminder.

Zipping along the wire, Donna felt anxiousness invading her body. That was something only God could heal.

Dear Lord, please don't let it rain or worse. I actually liked this. Please don't let me die on the last leg of this adventure. Wouldn't that be ironic? Thank you for helping me enjoy myself. Oh yeah, please make things between Joe and me clearer. He's doing too good of a job pretending, and my heart is breaking. Please give me wisdom.

Despite the impending weather, Donna's fear slowly vanished like the morning dew under a warm, rising sun. A breathless thought came over her. After everything, could she let Joe in as easily as she let her fear of zip-lining go?

By the time they reached their destination, Donna felt liberated. Heights still bothered her, but the feat she'd accomplished today spoke volumes about her ability to tackle the tough stuff.

"What a rush!" Andrea declared that once they were settled in the car, barely missing the rain. "We have a long
drive home. Let's play a game."

Donna sighed. "Your games get crazy. What are you
thinking?"

"Truth or Dare."

"No way."

"Scared?" Andrea looked over her shoulder, challenging
Donna with eyes.

Donna scoffed, "No."

"Great. Rules are: you can only do two truths in a row
before you have to say dare."

Both the men agreed quickly.

"Fine, I'm in," Donna stated dryly.

"Great, you can go first, Donna. Truth or Dare?" Andrea's
chipper voice sent a wave of irritation through Donna's
spine. She loved her friend, but sometimes. . .

"Truth."

Joe nudged a little closer. Not an easy thing for a big man
with a seat belt on. His attempt left her giddy like a teenager.
"Taking the easy way out. How bad could the dare be? We're
stuck in a car."

Donna lifted her eyebrows as if to say *don't challenge
Andrea.*

"What's the one thing you've never asked Joe to do but
really, really want to ask?"

Joe rubbed his palms together. "This is going to be a fun
game."

"You just wait until it's your turn," Donna retorted.

Donna was not prepared for this. She couldn't say what she really wanted — Joe to ask me out for real — so she better stick to something safe. "I've always wanted Joe to go running with me."

That was the truth, too.

Andrea scoffed, "Not interesting. Joe, your turn."

"Once we're married and you don't want to impress my mom any longer, you two are not playing games with each other," Brent announced.

He'd been referring to when Andrea met his parents for the first time and played games. According to Andrea, Brent's mom would give her a run for her money because she is just as competitive as Andrea.

"Truth," Joe cut into her thought.

"You two belong together. You're boring."

"We just zip-lined across three states. How is that boring?" Donna sounded a little prickly.

Andrea smiled, all sweet, but didn't answer her question. She knew Andrea just loved to play games, and she was harmless. Hackles down.

"Joe, what do you wish Donna would do for you?"

"Do for me?" Joe's cheeks pinked.

She'd never see him embarrassed. She hadn't thought it possible, but with a tinge of embarrassment, he was even more handsome; Donna silently swooned as the minutes ticked slowly.

"I wish Donna would give me a massage."

Heat slowly crept up her neck and face. She imagined it was more red than pink like Joe's had been. Donna couldn't imagine her hands massaging Joe's back and shoulders. The man's muscles were impressive, and her fingers pined to knead each ripple.

Andrea and Brent also revealed truths about each other — nothing that Donna and Joe didn't already know.

"Who's the boring one?" Donna teased. She'd never tell them, but they were the cutest couple ever.

During the next round of truths, Donna side-eyed Joe several times, catching him staring at her. What did that mean? She inhaled a deep breath, trying to calm every nerve ending firing throughout her body.

Thankfully, Brent drove. He tended to have a lead foot. "We're about forty minutes from the restaurant."

"Alright, Donna, you have to say dare now," Andrea snickered.

"Yup."

"I dare you to put your hand on any part of Joe and leave it there until we arrive at the restaurant."

"Seriously? Brent said we're about an hour away," Donna snapped.

"Choose wisely," Andrea shrugged.

Joe spread his arms wide, causing Donna to chuckle. "Slide on over, baby, make it easier on your back."

A light chortle escaped her. He hadn't been this bold in months.

Donna acted quickly, not wanting this to drag on, making her more embarrassed. She unbuckled, slid into the middle, buckled, and settled into Joe's shoulder. Her hand naturally rested on his abs. He sucked in a silent breath, making her grin. Their eyes met when she lifted her chin. Being this close gifted her the ability to see the gold flecks in his eyes. His dark blues dropped to her lips briefly before leaning forward.

Oh, my goodness. He's going to kiss me. Yes . . .No! Nerves caused her to turn forward, but he didn't stop progressing. His breath on her ear sent sparks of electricity down her spine, creating a fog in her brain; she'd never think clearly again.

"You look pretty in red," Joe whispered before kissing the spot right below her earlobe.

Ah, this was the Joe she'd missed — creating opportunities where they could connect.

The heat coming from her would have made anyone hot, yet she shivered. *Self-control, you have it.* She coached herself. *Actually, I don't. Lord, you make the rules, so give me the restraint I need to keep myself right with you.*

"You know you could have just held my hand. I find it interesting that you chose this." He gestured toward his abs.

He wasn't wrong. She hadn't thought of holding his hand. She lifted her body, but Joe pulled her close.

"Uh-Uh. You made your choice. Besides, you don't hear me complaining, do you?"

His playful voice made her smile.

She'd never wished time would stop and sped up simultaneously. When they arrived at their destination she would hug Andrea and then smack her for putting her in this situation.

Chapter 5

SHE MADE IT UNSCATHED through yesterday's car ride home. Fortunately, Brent kept Andrea occupied in conversation for the last forty-five minutes while she and Joe chatted in the back. He surprised her when he asked her to go golfing.

Again, something she'd never done, but at least her feet would be on the ground for this. As she drove to the course, guilt pricked at her insides. She knew her mom wasn't feeling well but kept her plans with Joe. Truthfully, she tried to cancel, but her mom refused. She kicked Donna out of the house and told her not to return until her date ended — much, much later — her words, not Donna's.

Her mom was never sick. She got a clean bill of health a few months back at her annual check-up, so her mom's recent illness baffled Donna.

More guilt filled Donna as she tried to keep her mind off Joe but couldn't. A flicker of wonder scratched at her insides. Why would he ask her to do something just for the two of them? Even through their fake dating, they were always with Brent and Andrea, except during their drives.

Her mom always said the good-looking ones were usually jerks, so they should be examined carefully. Saying Joe was good-looking was like saying the sky was blue. He had ex-quisite features, with gorgeous blue eyes, tousled hair, and rough stubble. However, Donna saw a vulnerability in him whenever he spoke of his dad.

Maybe today, she could get to the bottom of his game. He either wanted to dissolve their dating agreement, or he didn't. It doesn't seem like a difficult concept. Why do men have to make everything so complicated?

She parked in the front row of the country club. She had never been here before. No surprise there. This place reeked of money. Her mom worked two jobs just to get her through high school. Though Donna took out student loans and put herself through college, her mom continued working but saved her money. She always said, "I'll need it someday."

This place reminded her of the country club in Dirty Dancing. It had lush, manicured lawns and white tents strategically placed throughout its endless acres. Where's Johnny and Baby?

"They have off today."

Donna whipped around. Apparently, she said that last part out loud, given the smirk on Joe's sun-kissed face. Why did he have to be so appealing?

"Ready to play?" Joe reached for her hand, "Come on, Baby?"

"Okay, Johnny," Donna giggled.

Joe blew out a huff of air. "Oh, no. I can't dance."

"At all, or like *that?*"

"I plead the fifth."

"Interesting."

At the first hole, Joe motioned for her to begin. He set her stance, and then the cool spring day disappeared. A blazing July sun fired throughout her body when Joe wrapped his taut arms around her, meticulously placing her hands on the club, and settling his on top of her grasp. The black grip did nothing to prevent her slick hands from sliding down the club.

"Keep a firm grip." Joe tightened his hands around hers. She knew he wasn't whispering sweet nothings in her ear but rather giving her instructions, like a coach. But her body responded as if his low, husky voice was the cherry on top of her ice cream sundae.

His upper body pressed against her back, keeping her focus on *him* and not the small round ball he'd instructed her to focus on. His biceps enveloped her petite frame as he brought her arms back for the swing. She felt the force from his muscular upper body that she would have never been able to replicate.

The ball landed about twenty feet from the hole.

"Alright, look at you. You're a natural."

Yeah right! It was his delicious strength and force that made her seem successful.

When she looked, his jaw slacked. "What's wrong?"

"You think I have delicious strength?"

"What? No. What would make you think that?"

His smug smile pulled at his mouth. "Because you just said it."

"In my out loud voice?"

"Yup. Can't take it back now."

"Great, I've created an arrogant monster."

"Not likely."

Joe helped her through the remaining seventeen holes. Donna got the hang of the stance and even the swing but botched her attempt when he had her try it alone, so he'd continued with his assistance. It was a sweet torture she wasn't ready to give up. After this outing, she knew her heart was all Joe's, and she didn't have anyone except herself to blame for the pain that came her way. Everyone said the heart was resilient; it would bounce back. Is that still the case even when someone shatters it?

Chapter 6

J OE'S CHEST FILLED WITH angst. He shoved his phone in his pocket. Of course, his mom had told him to bring Donna over for dinner this week. How would that work? Since their golf date, they'd only interacted at work—by interacting, he meant flirted.

Since Donna had mentioned that she liked his physique, he'd taken every opportunity to show it off by flexing his muscles whenever he'd lifted anything in her presence. However, he still hadn't expressed his feelings to her, yet. Didn't she know? It seemed obvious to him. The last thing he wanted to do was hurt her.

Per usual, Joe had stuck his foot in his mouth, and like all the other times, he didn't know how to remove it.

"When will I stop disappointing people?" Joe asked the empty room.

"What did you do now, and how much will it cost?" Brent strolled out of his office.

Startled, Joe snickered. "You know me. Trouble calls my name, and I answer. Every. Single. Time.

Before Brent could ask any more questions, Joe shoved a box in his direction. "Help me unpack this inventory, would ya?"

"What's the rush?" Brent asked, pushing the box back in Joe's direction.

It may have seemed unusual to unpack the equipment they ordered in the off-season this early, but Joe couldn't focus on anything else right now.

He rubbed his hands together like he was preparing to dig into a long-awaited meal. *Rippp.* Joe pulled the tape off the first box. With the same energy, he ripped open the rest of the boxes. He wouldn't admit it out loud, but opening the merchandise reminded Joe of the open wound at the center of his chest.

Brent shook his head. "I guess we're doing this?" He bent over, lifting the laps on the first box. As he pulled out the first harness, inspecting its quality, he inquired, "What's been up with you the last month?"

Joe coughed, choking on his saliva. "I'm not sure what you mean."

"You mope around when you're here. Whenever I ask if you want to catch a bite to eat, you give me a lame excuse for rejecting my offer. You and Donna haven't been out with Andrea and me for weeks."

Great. He had noticed. Joe had unintentionally suggested that he and Donna dissolve their fake relationship agreement. For a brief moment, he'd thought disappointment had filled her eyes, but then she agreed, crushing Joe to pieces.

Their last day in Hawaii hadn't gone well after that. Stunned, Donna had agreed to skydive. Her fear of heights ran deep. Once she landed, Joe had helped her take off her harness just as her stomach had rebelled against the adventure. He'd handed her towels, offering his help. She had graciously taken them but quickly dismissed him. She seemed so fragile after losing her breakfast. Joe had wanted to wrap her up and declare that he'd misspoken. In his mind, telling Brent and Andrea they'd faked their relationship hadn't been an option. Why? He'd forgotten it was fake.

"It's a busy time. I've been working on the new website designs we planned. Donna's been crunching our first quarter numbers." Joe rubbed his hand along his jaw, feeling the short stubble he'd let grow out the last thirty days. "People are starting to notice us. We've sold a ridiculous amount of season passes."

You'll never be successful at that park. His dad's hurtful comments replayed in his mind.

"Donna told me the figures earlier." Brent rested his arms across his chest. "None of this explains your withdrawal."

The mere mention of her name made Joe's throat go dry. She'd avoided him ever since they returned from Hawaii. He doubted she would eat dinner with him and his parents, but that didn't stop the mountain–sized desire growing in his chest.

"We're having dinner with my parents this week, but we'll get together with you and Andrea soon, okay?" Perhaps both of those statements would turn out to be lies. If it appeased Brent at the moment, Joe would figure out the details later.

"Yeah, that works." the arch in his brow told Joe that Brent wasn't convinced.

The bell above the door rang, jerking Joe's head in that direction. He forced the harness in his hand on the metal arm before abandoning the rest on the floor. Jogging toward Donna, he took the oversized box from her arms. *Oh, goodness,* Joe's knees buckled slightly.

"How many people do you have in here?"

"Funny." Donna chuckled, setting the bags on the counter.

Joe couldn't help but notice her eyes roaming over his flexed biceps. *Too bad I couldn't hold his box forever,* he mused, walking toward the middle of the room. He knelt slowly, bending at the knees. He set the box gently on the floor, half concerned about the contents.

"Thank you for picking that up, Donna," declared Brent, walking toward his friends.

"No problem. I'm going to finish my paperwork. I'll get you the final figures before I leave unless you need anything else?"

"We're good, Donna. Thank you." Brent nodded his head.

Once her door closed, Brent backhanded Joe across the chest. "See. That's what I'm talking about, cried Brent, extending his hand toward the space Donna retreated.

"I mess everything up. You know that." Maybe *everything* was a bit of an exaggeration, but Joe had ruined his relationship with his parents - at least his dad, and now he'd loved and lost his *fake* girlfriend. That sounded absurd - fake girlfriend - who messes up something fake? Joe Hartley, that's who.

Brent touched Joe's shoulder, "I'll take care of this. It's a bunch of wedding presents from my parents. Sending them made more sense than flying them or buying them when they arrived." With both men standing at full height, Brent put his other hand on Joe's shoulder, forcing his friend to focus on his words. "You can fix this. It's clear that Donna makes you happy. Don't let your past dictate your future."

He snapped his fingers in front of Joe's eyes. "Are you with me?"

Joe found Brent's words inspiring yet terrifying. His feelings for Donna seemed to grow stronger every day. Right now, his body appeared calm and relaxed despite the mental picture of Donna moments ago. His mind wasn't focusing on the skin-tight exercise pants wrapped around Donna's legs. Nor was his heart racing from the long-sleeved running shirt that covered her hips and snugged to her firm abs.

The closer he moved toward his imminent demise, known as the closed office door, the more sweat beads formed at his hairline. His heart raced faster than Usain Bolt in the hundred-meter sprint. The thermostat reflected that Brent and Joe ran hot. But the lava bubbling inside Joe had nothing to do with the room's temperature. The woman on the other side of the door—

Joe and Donna both jumped when she whipped open the door, paperwork in hand. "Joe." Her voice high as she looked up at him.

"Hey. Can we talk?"

She stepped back into the office. Joe said a quick prayer for the right words so he wouldn't sound like an idiot.

Donna leaned against the desk. The baggy sweatshirt she'd thrown on couldn't save him from thoughts he'd repent later. Donna couldn't hide her beauty. He saw her long, slender neck - one he fantasized about trailing kisses down. For months, he'd wanted to kiss Donna — really kiss her. Sure, he'd kissed her cheek or hand, but the urge to kiss her full, rose-bud-colored lips had taken up residency in his brain.

"Aren't you hot?" Joe blurted out to fill the tense silence.

"You said I was before, but that's obviously not the case anymore." Donna deadpanned. Something akin to a punch in the gut struck his soul.

What have I done to her? Emotion oozed from her eyes. Unfortunately, Joe recognized her feelings—hurt, despair, and perhaps disgust. Joe had never been lucky with the ladies. Every time he thought the girl liked him, they'd only used him—term papers, a study partner, whatever they needed. Her eyes reflected the same pain he'd experienced. *She thinks I used her.*

She crossed her arms over her chest, trapping her wavy blonde hair that cascaded over her shoulders. "What did you want to talk about?"

His eyes softened, unsure how to proceed. If he asked her to dinner, she'd be convinced he used her. If he tried to explain himself, he'd look like an idiot and hurt her more.

"Joe?"

He stepped closer, hoping she wouldn't push him away. He reached for her hand. "I miss your smile, your laugh. Hanging out and watching movies isn't the same without you."

Her eyes pooled with tears. Joe's determination to fix this ramped up. "Donna, I misspoke in Hawaii. I didn't want to tell Brent and Andrea about faking dating—

The phone rang, startling them both. After a few more rings, Donna answered it.

Brent, you're supposed to be helping me out. Where are you?

"You're going to be busy this summer. That camp booked for the entire day. . . one hundred seventy-five guests."

Joe didn't want to talk about the business right now, though that was a great booking. He grabbed her hand and pulled her into a hug. He rested his hands just below her shoulder blades. Reluctantly, she wrapped her arms around his lower back, gripping his shirt. Her body was as stiff as the mountain he'd climbed last weekend.

Just a few inches shorter than his six-three frame, Donna's hot breath grazed his neck, sending bubbling lava through his veins.

You smell good.

"I'm glad you think so, but did you really pull me from work to discuss how I smell?" Donna pulled away slightly.

Joe slapped his forehead. "I'm sorry. I didn't realize I said that out loud."

"What else is your not out loud voice saying?" her lips slowly curved into a smile.

"You don't want to know." Joe huffed out a laugh.

Her lips curled at either side of her perfectly shaped mouth. Was she flirting with him? No. The expression on her face revealed a pure satisfaction that being this close to her was torture.

"I hope you can forgive me. Maybe we can start over?"

She opened her mouth to respond, but the door flew open. Brent. *Come on, Dude. You're killing me.*

"Everything good in here? What day are you two eating with your parents? Andrea insisted the four of us go to dinner this week, too."

I'm going to kill him! Donna's eyes lost their sparkle. She put miles between them physically — he instantly felt the chill. Brent seemed to notice the change in demeanor also, causing him to shut the door slowly. He caught my eye and mouthed, *sorry.*

Donna retreated behind her desk. "What day are your parents expecting us?" her tone somber.

"Mom said to let her know." Joe choked out the response.

"I can do any night except Tuesday. You and Brent can fig-ure out the day that works with Andrea." She pretended to work on her computer, but she'd already said she finished. "I'll be there to keep up this charade, but right now, I need to get back to work." Her eyes stayed glued to the computer screen.

Her pain stabbed his heart. He'd hurt her again. *Come on, Lord, what is wrong with me?*

Joe wouldn't blame Brent for interrupting. Talking with girls, especially the pretty ones, had always intimidated Joe.

Donna's beauty was only the beginning. She was intelligent and entertaining. He'd grown accustomed to having her around. Like a fool, he opened his mouth and ruined everything — twice.

Yeah, Donna withdrew after Brent left the office, but Joe clammed up himself. He couldn't handle the pain in Donna's eyes, especially knowing he put it there.

His feet finally moved toward the door. Was it inappropriate to ask what she was doing on Tuesday? Probably. But it tortured him not knowing.

Joe got what he wanted — Donna agreed to have dinner with his parents — so why did it feel like he'd lost?

Chapter 7

♥

Donna arrived early for work. The park didn't open until nine, so it was rare for any guys to arrive before seven-thirty. Settling in her chair with her water bottle, she pulled her laptop from its case and lifted the lid.

Donna found it easier to focus when Joe wasn't around. Just knowing he was in the building caused her emotions to go haywire. She hoped their zip-lining adventure had brought them closer, but the reality was far from it. The strain of maintaining a facade in front of Brent was taking its toll on her.

Today, her heart might get a reprieve from seeing Joe since she needed to take her mom to the doctor. She hadn't been feeling well lately and claimed her body itched all over. Donna couldn't put her finger on it, but something drastic affected her mom.

Feeling alarmed, Donna made her mom schedule an appointment. She knew something wasn't right. Her mom didn't have an appetite, and she'd lost weight. This only came on after her mom's physical three months ago. Forcing herself to remain positive, Donna prayed. *Lord, up until now, Mom has been healthy. Please give us answers. I have a sickening feeling about this whole situation. Please enlighten me.*

For weeks, every night after work, Donna cooked dinner for her mom — sometimes she ate it, sometimes she didn't — and stayed with her until she fell asleep. "I should just move back in and save rent," Donna said aloud last night while cleaning up. Depending on what the doctor said, she might do just that.

Focus! Donna silently ordered. She felt helpless and confused. What could be making her mom feel this way?

Emily Greer was a strong, tough woman. She raised her daughter on her own after Donna turned two and her dad bolted. She exercised four to six times a week, often running with Donna. They hadn't run together for more than two months. Seeing her mom weak, Donna knew something big had to be wrong.

Despite her distraction, Donna was finishing the payroll for the week when a knock rumbled through her office door. Her stomach plummeted like a skydive gone wrong, and she prayed quickly that it wasn't Joe.

"Come in," Donna's voice hitched.

The door flung open. Brent leaned on the knob while holding on to the door jamb. *That would look so much better if it had been Joe. Stop it!*

"What time are you leaving today? I was hoping you could go over the first quarter results." Donna suspected Brent's cheery tone was related to Andrea and their wedding plans.

She had watched him transform over the last eight months and was so happy for her friends.

"I can show you now if you want." She heard the bell over the main entrance ring. That must be Joe, her double-crossing stomach doing a backflip.

Truthfully, her entire body enjoyed Joe's proximity. He owned more real estate in her heart and mind than a Monopoly winner. But she hurt more when reality seeped in, which it always did.

Brent waved Joe into the office and dragged chairs on either side of her. Donna worked to get the software open as Brent sat next to her.

Seconds later, Joe appeared in the doorway. Even though Donna had been mentally prepared, her already stressed mind went blank. Her fingers froze in the ready position above her keyboard, and her pulse quickened.

Joe had teased her about only liking Infinity Wars because of Thor. Little did Joe know, his piercing blue eyes put Chris Hemsworth's to shame. Her eyes were glued to him as he whipped off his sweatshirt revealing the short sleeves hugging his biceps. The casual toss of his hoodie onto the chair in front of her desk certainly didn't help settle her pulse.

Oh, God, help me.

Joe caught her ogling him. With his shoulders down and back, he pushed out his chest and swaggered to the free chair, which was considerably closer to Donna's than Brent's.

Man, Joe oozed confidence right now. Who was he trying to impress? It certainly wasn't Brent and he'd called it quits on dating her in Hawaii, so maybe he was practicing for his next girlfriend. Her heart cringed.

Joe wrapped an arm around her shoulders and kissed her on the temple. "Mornin' beautiful." That simple touch, one she knew was a sham — part of his role in the fake dating charade — tilted her stomach on its axis.

She'd never experienced any feeling remotely close to this. Whenever her mom talked about the early days with Donna's dad, she told her that butterflies constantly invaded her belly at the slightest brush. Donna's *butterflies* felt like hawk wings flapping wildly.

Thinking about her dad left her with a hole the size of Maine in her heart. She'd been a toddler when he'd abandoned her, so she didn't have a clue how to read men. Donna didn't have any confidence in her mom's counsel on the subject, either, considering how her relationship had turned out.

The last time Donna dated anyone, he left just like her dad. After college graduation, Rick accused her of 'never being all in,' so he left.

Donna shook off the memory and leaned away from the falseness of Joe's safe, warm embrace. What did a few more memorable touches matter? Joe left her, too. The worst part was that Donna had really fallen for him. His sweetness — picking flowers for her and putting them behind her ear. His kindness — offering her a towel after she lost her breakfast skydiving the first time. His protectiveness — staying with her during every adventure until she finished.

"So here's your 10-Q filings for the first quarter. The marketing we did in the first two months of the year worked. You're up twelve percent from last year at this time."

"Look at those numbers, Brent Baby. We are on our way!" Joe rubbed his hands together. Dear ole Dad shouldn't complain when I tell him about this."

"But he will," Brent declared matter-of-factly.

Joe's shoulders slumped, causing Donna to frown. She met his sad eyes. He'd mentioned his hypercritical father in passing but changed the subject quickly. Donna had only met him briefly at Thanksgiving. The man left his family to address a work issue. It's not like he was a doctor. Why were people working at a construction site on Thanksgiving anyway?

Brent's cell phone buzzed. He excused himself.

All the pain and hurt she'd felt for Joe that holiday rushed back. She saw the desire to please his dad in his eyes. "I'm sorry your dad makes you feel like you're not enough."

Our eyes froze on each other's. Time crawled until she continued. "You need to know that you are everything. . . to us."

Donna closed her programs and shut her lid. She was confused by the emotions rippling through her body. What did Joe mean to her? Her brain beeped like a warning sound: Stay away. Leave before he leaves you, for real. Yet, her heart softened for him. How could his father basically disown him?

Chapter 8

♥

JOE GRABBED HIS POLO shirt and pulled it over his head. He should be focused on what his dad would throw at him and how he would respond.

Instead, he couldn't stop thinking about Donna. Everything about her grabbed his attention. He'd be lying if he said he wasn't physically drawn to her. He imagined every man would find her appealing. If he didn't let her know it soon, one of those men would come and swoop her up like one had with every other girl he'd ever shown interest in.

So why bother fussing over his appearance? For her. Whenever he let his hair air dry, it looked messy, irritating his dad, but Andrea let it slip one day that Donna liked it that way. He hasn't touched the blow dryer since.

Joe knew he had issues to get past. Everyone had baggage. Her words, 'You're everything to us,' settled in his mind. Did she really mean that? Could they ever have a life together? One that wasn't based on a lie.

Only if he could get a grip on his insecurity. He'd graduated high school Valedictorian, which attributed to the extreme pressure his father inflicted upon him. 'Be first. That will make you richer than me someday.' His dad's words felt like hot acid burning his throat.

Only Ivan Hartley, the millionaire engineer, AKA Dad, cared about status and bank accounts. Joe had graduated from his dad's Alma mater at the top of his class, but after earning his engineering degree, he disappointed his dad by entering the business world.

It was the best defining moment in his life — breaking free from the ropes he let his father strangle him with for years. Sadly, he doesn't feel free!

Not like he did when he was in the great wide open or at the summit of a mountain. Would he feel better letting his dad know he and Brent were quickly building a multi-million dollar company? Based on Donna's numbers, they projected to reach that status in two years.

Joe oversaw every renovation, designed the new structures they'd added since their takeover, and planned new thrills for the following season.

Despite what his father thought, Joe used his engineering degree, just not for his dad. He avoided khaki pants, a dress shirt, and a tie for work. Instead, he wore whatever athletic clothing he felt like. Most often, it was whatever would make that day's adventure most effortless.

The alarm on his phone jolted him from his thoughts. "Let's get this over with," he said to no one.

"*Only five more minutes?* Ugh!" Donna exclaimed to her reflection in the mirror, her fingers trembling uncontrollably as she tried to mask the dark circles under her eyes. Like a relentless drum, her heart pounded in her chest, threatening to burst out. An uneasy knot twisted and turned in her stomach, a physical manifestation of her anxiety. Why was she so obsessed with looking perfect? She was about to admit to Joe's parents she was never his *real* girlfriend. Her eyes blurred. An uneasiness gnawed at her the same way it did as she lay in bed every night, keeping her awake.

It'd been eight months since she'd agreed with Joe that fake dating was the only way their friends would spend more time together. Over that time, Joe and Donna had interacted nearly every day in some fashion. Their late-night texting sessions filled her heart with appreciation for Joe and a hint of something more.

He'd refrained from giving her too many details about himself, but he'd encouraged her. She'd always wondered if he'd been flirting with her. Clearly, that hadn't been the case. He'd been fulfilling the role of fake boyfriend - *very well.* He hadn't acted much differently whether they were around others or not. Unfortunately, her heart, against her will, had started to develop a romantic attraction, a feeling she couldn't control.

She washed the concealer from her hands, her heart in her throat. The sound of the doorbell echoed through the house, breaking the silence. *Ding-dong.*

Donna tugged on the bottom hem of her shirt and looked in the mirror. "That's as good as it gets." She slowly walked to the door, praying aloud. "Lord, give me the words to get through the night. Protect and guard my heart."

Her shaky hands gripped the doorknob. Donna slowly turned the handle, and her eyes locked on the most handsome man she'd ever seen. Joe wasn't a big guy like Dwayne Johnson, but Joe's solid frame had muscles on top of muscles. Donna had seen him shirtless in Hawaii, and while that beautiful picture still lived vividly in her mind, The image standing before her parched her throat. She felt her mouth drop slightly as he handed her a bouquet of multicolored tulips, his bicep and tricep working together in harmony.

The corners of Joe's mouth turned slightly upward. The smug look told Donna that he saw the attraction written on her face. "Can I come in, or do you want to get headed?"

"C-come in." Donna sputtered, reaching for the flowers. "Thank you. Do I have a minute to put them in water?"

"Take all the time you need. We're the special guest, so dinner won't start without us," Joe quipped.

She reached for the vase on the top shelf of her cupboard but came up short.

"Here, let me get that," Joe quick-stepped, not giving her time to move. His chest pressed against her back, and the warmth from his breath melted her insides, "Sorry," his husky whisper, reflecting the opposite of his spoken word, as he reached over her head, grabbed the vase, and handed it to her. He lingered at her back long enough to set the vase on the counter. Then, just like that, he returned to the door. Had that just happened? Was her fantasizing confusing reality?

Donna's mind continued to race. *Hopefully, God would come through with protection for tonight. He must have missed the request for help talking to the man she'd fallen for yet couldn't be with. Lord, don't let me imagine things that aren't happening, and give me the strength to be under the same roof as this man.*

Ever since Joe had dropped the bombshell on Donna in Hawaii, he'd inundated her with mixed signals. She didn't blame him. Their fake dating had an expiration date. She couldn't help but think her heart hadn't received the memo. Until she'd sent him away, Joe had caressed her back and given her towels after her skydiving adventure. He'd brought her lunch at work. It hadn't mattered that they worked in the same office; he'd thought of her, causing her stomach to flip-flop in his presence.

"Ready." Donna choked out. She didn't know how she'd get through this night without telling the truth. She could not pretend she didn't have feelings for him.

Chapter 9

IT SEEMED LIKE DONNA blinked, and they'd arrived at his parent's house. His delicious, musky scent filled the cab of the truck, clogging her brain and preventing her from forming any cohesive sentences the entire ride. "Ah, we never talked about what we were going to say," Donna sputtered.

Killing the engine, Joe studied her. The lazy sun cast a shadow across Joe's face, making it nearly impossible for Donna to read his thoughts. "I'll do whatever you want."

He'd already stolen her heart. She knew exactly what she wanted.

Don't be a fool! Follow the expectation. This had been a plan of the minds, but she'd willingly given her heart to him.

Big. Big. Problem. He hadn't been falling in love with her. He was playing a part. She liked his starring role - the hunky boyfriend doting on his girlfriend - one that would win him an Oscar.

"If we're going to dissolve the relationship, then we need to either come clean with them now, or you need to tell them after you take me home tonight."

Did he just frown?

Joe hopped out of the truck without missing a beat and jogged to her side. He held his strong, calloused hand out for Donna. Nervous energy buzzed around them. It would be impossible to reign in her heart while touching him. Was physical contact necessary?

Yet again, her head lost the battle. Donna's heart reached out and grabbed Joe's hand. Upon contact, bursts of electricity tingled through her fingers, *and something akin to the pop* of a transformer exploded in her belly. This man was her kryptonite.

"Relax," Joe whispered, leaning into her head. He brushed his lips over her temple.

What the heck? Donna felt dizzy. Her obituary would read: Donna Greer ate dinner with her once fake boyfriend, turned heartbreaker, who kissed her on the side of the head, and she died. *Oh, brother!*

The last few steps toward the door filled Donna with apprehension. "This is going to be a disaster." She began, barely above a whisper. "I mean, we're not dating. You don't even want me around."

Joe's eyes softened. He pulled Donna closer to him, "You have to understand. I—"

"Oh, look at the happy couple," Joe's mom flung open the door, halting Joe's words.

Donna's arms hesitantly wrapped around Joe's mom upon her open-arm request. Pulling back, Donna ran her fingers through her hair, which was cascading over her face. She sighed, pushing it out of her eyes. When Joe muttered, "Let's get this over with."

"Mrs. Hartley, you keep this house immaculate. Mr. Hartley's an engineer, right? I guess they do pretty well for themselves." Donna realized how inappropriate that sounded, but the smile on Beverly's face remained solidly in place. Hopefully, Donna hadn't offended her.

"Yes, we do." Mr. Hartley's robust voice filled the entryway.

Donna startled. Joe gently pulled her to his side as if he genuinely cared that someone had jumped her.

"Oh, Mr. Hartley, it's. a pleasure to see you again." Donna never lied, but tension from their first meeting still troubled her.

For once, the tension in the room wasn't hers but Joe's. He seemed very uncomfortable around his dad. She'd asked Joe about it before. "We don't see eye-to-eye." Well, that could have been more helpful. There could be a million things they don't see the same. By Joe's tight squeeze on her waist, she sensed she'd find out tonight.

"Welcome to our home, Donna. Bev and I are happy to have you." Mr. Hartley was a natural actor like his son. This tone revealed the truth — having dinner with her had not been his idea. He certainly didn't want her in his home.

"Let's eat," Beverly interjected.

"Can we help set the table?" Donna offered.

"Nope. Everything is done. We were waiting on the two of you." Mr. Hartley answered for his wife.

Why had I agreed to this? Donna had friends who hated their childhood because their fathers made them feel unimportant and belittled. This was new territory for Donna. Her dad had deserted her. At one time, she'd wished she had a dad to belittle her just so she'd have someone to call *Dad*. Mr. Hartley made her feel grateful real quick that she never got what she'd wished for.

Including both meetings, she'd only been in Mr. Hartley's presence for about thirty minutes, but she now understood what type of fathers her friends had been talking about. Poor Joe.

As she followed Joe's mom, Donna gaped at the curing staircase leading to the second floor. The white cathedral ceilings made Donna feel minuscule. Absent-mindedly, she ran her fingertips gently over the small table in the middle of the entryway, which held a large vase with freshly cut flowers.

"Here we are," Bev led Donna into a room furnished with three love seats and four fancy-looking, high-backed chairs strategically placed around a perfectly polished cherry table. A fireplace on the inside wall looked too clean to have been used lately, and floor-to-ceiling windows spanned the outside wall.

Small talk between Beverly and Joe warmed Donna's heart. Their love showed in their soft tones and laughter. She might be imagining things again, but she heard the same softness in his voice when he spoke with her. The conversation with his dad sounded different.

Mr. Hartley put his fork and knife in an x position at the center of his plate. "Son, when will you give up your silly adventures and get a real job?"

Donna felt the tension radiate from Joe's body. Her frustration sky-rocketed. *How dare his dad discourage him?* Donna did the books. She knew how successful their business — their *career* — had been this first quarter alone. Their previous fourth-quarter sales had doubled from last year's. That's when the company had been closed for the season. She knew this would be their year.

"Do we have to get into this now?" Joe's gritted answer matched Donna's frustration.

"Yes, we do. You're an engineer. You've got a degree, one I paid for, in case you forgot, and you're wasting it."

A patch of red crept up Joe's neck. In another couple of months, his tan would hide his anger easily. Donna placed her palm on Joe's forearm. Maybe it would bring him some comfort. "

"I'm proud of you, Dad, for creating a successful business. You have more engineers working for you than Disney. I'm glad you reached your goal, but I do not have any interest in working for you."

Joe's honesty struck Donna. She knew that Joe didn't argue with his dad often. Void of desire to argue with his flesh and blood, he chose the verbal lashing.

"As a matter of fact. I know exactly how much you paid for my degree. Let me start paying you back for that."

Calmy, Mr. Hartley steepled his fingers while leaning back in his chair. "That's not what I'm suggesting."

"No, of course not. Then you wouldn't have anything you can hold against me."

Donna snuck a peek at Beverly. Her somber demeanor told Donna this wasn't the first battle between the Hartley men. Like Donna, Joe's mom had barely eaten, but both women gave up trying when Mr. Hartley started this battle.

"When I was your age," Mr. Hartley started, leaning forward. Simultaneously, Joe dropped his fork on his plate, producing a loud clang that jumped Donna.

Joe rested his palm on her thigh. She interlaced their fingers and gently squeezed them. He caressed her skin with his thumb. The sparks of electricity burning the skin under his touch briefly took her from the conversation.

"Don't you want that, Son?"

"Eventually, yes."

What did Joe want eventually? Donna forced her brain to focus on the conversation and not her feelings for the handsome man holding her hand.

"You've never had a girlfriend longer than a month. How do you expect to get a girl worth marrying living in an apartment?" Mr. Hartley's dark eyes landed on Donna. "No offense, dear. I'm not insinuating anything."

The obligatory smile slowly spreading across his face infuriated Donna. How dare this arrogant man insult his son and now her!?

"That's enough," Joe raised his voice, catching his mother's attention. "You can put me down and run your mouth about me. But don't you ever direct your comments toward Donna," Joe slid his chair back.

Finally, they could leave this dinner party. Too bad Beverly couldn't come with him. Donna assumed she struggled with her husband's mindset.

"Hold up. All I'm saying is the plan was for you to get your degree and work for me. Getting a house and tying the knot was the next step. Your mother wants grandchildren. I put you through school. You haven't held up your end of the bargain - I can't get your house and your woman for you. That's up to you."

Donna had heard enough. His son's life wasn't some business deal to negotiate. With a tight chest, she stood abruptly, tipping the chair on its back legs. Thankfully, Joe's quick reflexes caught and grounded it before it could fall. "Thank you so much, Beverly, for dinner."

Donna whipped her head toward Mr. Hartley. "Who do you think created the designs for Adventure for You? Joe poured his heart and soul into the creation of everything at the park. How do you know Joe isn't waiting to let his wife pick out the house she'll live in for the rest of her life? I'm sorry I am a disappointment — clearly not who you'd pick out for your son, but it doesn't matter who *you'd* pick. Joe's an intelligent man. When he's ready, he'll get married and have a house. Maybe it won't be as elaborate as this one. Do you like your house, Mr. Hartley?"

"Of course."

"Do you like it for its features or for what it says about you?" Donna didn't wait for his response. Based on his pursed lips, he got the point. "Joe could afford a house bigger than this one based on the park's first quarter sales alone, and the park hasn't even opened yet. You're so concerned about Joe finding a wife and starting a family. Have you ever wondered if *you're* the reason that hasn't happened yet?"

Donna's adrenaline started to fade. Embarrassment began to creep in, and Donna slowly returned to her seat. She captured Beverly's attention, who gave her a faint head nod.

"Ivan, can't you just let Joe live his life?"

"Beverly! You need to back me up on this! He isn't living up to his end of the deal!" Mr. Hartley slammed his fist on the table.

Unable to sit, Ivan shot out of his seat, pointing at Joe. "Maybe that's why you haven't had a girlfriend that long. They have to fight your battles for you. That must be tiring."

"I'd venture a guess other girls didn't want to deal with you, and Joe had to pay the price." Donna challenged.

Joe sprang to his feet, pulling Donna out of her sweet with him. "Time to go. Sorry, Mom. We'd help pick up, but I think it's best we leave."

Oh no, she crossed the line. Would Joe ever forgive her? She'd never been in a situation like this before. Donna had never told anyone off before, especially someone's dad. Even though they weren't even fake dating — heck, Donna didn't know if they were even friends — she should have let him fight his own battles.

Her heart picked up speed, watching Joe round the front of the truck. Always a gentleman, Joe opened her door. He didn't touch the small of her back like he had at her house. He didn't cup her elbow like when they arrived at his parents. She'd seriously ticked him off. She didn't blame him. She could only imagine how she'd feel if Joe let loose on her mom like she had his dad.

Joe put the truck in reverse. Reaching for his belt, he secured the buckle and pulled onto the main road.

Joe and Donna spoke at the same time. "Thank you." "I'm so sorry."

She picked at the skin on the back of her hand. "Why did you thank me?"

"No one has ever stood up for me like that. Not to my dad, anyway. Brent helped at school, but my dad's always been a beast." He reached out, wrapping his fingers around hers, preventing her from tearing her skin off. "Why are you sorry?"

"We were supposed to tell them we're not dating. Your dad made me so angry." She stopped herself from saying, "No one will talk about my man that way." If only Joe were her man.

"Change of subject. Brent and I are hiking tomorrow morning, so one of the employees will open the store."

"Okay. I have an appointment tomorrow morning. Brent told me I could work from home."

Joe pulled into her driveway. "Why have you been avoiding me?"

Duh! It's too hard being around you. "If we're supposed to dissolve, spending so much time together doesn't make sense for us or those watching."

Without saying a word, Joe exited the truck's cab. Seconds later, he opened her door and silently held out his hand. His dreamy, blue eyes pulled her from the seat. Her hand fit perfectly inside Joe's rough, larger-than-life hand.

Her heel caught on the floor mat. She broke their gaze, reaching for the door. Warm zings spiderwebbed through her elbow when Joe tenderly wrapped his fingers around the joint, forcing her to freeze inches away from his face. "Thank you," she whispered.

"You look gorgeous tonight," Donna's insides squealed, taking in Joe's four words. Joe tugged her closer and shut the truck door, jolting her back to reality. He couldn't keep playing with her mind.

"Ah, you don't have to waste those comments now; no one is around," Donna said casually.

"I don't say things for anyone else's benefit, " his low, husky voice made her heart pitter-patter. He took a half-step clos-er. Her breath hitched as he closed the gap between his lips and her cheek. "You're a beautiful woman, Donna - on the inside and out." His lips gently pressed against her cheek, sending a pleasant reverberation through her body.

She couldn't look at him. The minute their eyes met, Don-na knew her resolve would disappear. "Thank you."

"Thank you for keeping our secret," Joe said, walking her to the door. "Are you still okay going out with Brent and Andrea at the end of the week?"

"Yes." She lied. How much longer could her heart take Joe's fake affection?

Chapter 10

♥

J OE'S PHONE BLARED ON the nightstand, jarring him from his restless sleep. A text from Brent awaited him.

Are you ready? I'm outside waiting.

Ugh. Six o'clock came early. Joe's eyelid had finally given in at about three. After punching his pillow, talking at his ceiling, and pacing the floor, his exhausted body finally relented.

Throwing his covers off, Joe swung his legs over the edge of the bed, and his feet landed on the floor.

Sorry. Be out in five.

Thank God I packed last night. Joe couldn't wait to breathe in the fresh mountain air and discuss things with Brent. They'd been friends since Kindergarten. Brent stuck up for him against mean kids and assured him when every girl used him and then dumped him.

Joe's impulsivity hindered his success more than it benefited him. His situation with Donna was the latest example. Surprisingly, Joe had kept the fake dating secret from Brent, something he'd never done before. It would be a miracle if Joe only vented about his dad. In reality, he needed advice regarding Donna.

Should he send Donna a quick text? Keeping the truth from their friends was his idea. Would Donna be upset if he discussed it with Brent without her knowledge?

After brushing his teeth and tossing his dirty clothes in the hamper, Joe dressed in hiking pants. He tied his hiking boots and grabbed his pack, securing it on his back. He retrieved his protein shake from the refrigerator and left.

"It's about time." Brent tossed his playful words from the opened driver's side door.

"I didn't sleep. Sorry."

"You look like something the cat dragged in. Wanna talk about it?"

What a loaded question. If they talked about his dad — the only thing he should probably discuss — Joe wouldn't feel any relief. His dad didn't affect his feelings. He wasn't sure when it happened, but Joe avoided or ignored his dad's rants criticizing his life choices. That seemed like a better solution than fighting with the man who'd raised him. Donna, on the other hand, encompassed all his emotions. Recently, he'd imagined the two of them married. They'd ride to work together, sneak kisses in her office, and instead of walking in the house together at the end of the day, he'd go in before her and greet her with a toe-curling kiss that would lead into an indoor recreation before they made dinner together.

"Joe!" Brent's stern voice jumped him, bringing him back to reality. "It must be awful. Did you and Donna break up?"

His head whipped toward Brent, and he pulled his door shut at the same time. "What would make you say that?" Joe snapped.

Brent put his hands up in surrender. "Whoa, there, Killer. Nothing ever bothers you, and today, you're like a caged lion scratching at the gate."

"Sorry, Man." Joe rubbed his palm against his beard. Something he'd grown after Donna commented on a little facial hair being hot. He rested his head back against the rest and grunted.

He shut his eyes, and the night they'd made their fake dating arrangement flooded to the forefront. It was a luke-warm August evening. He'd been hoping for an actual date but couldn't get the words — some things never change. A smile slowly formed on his face as he remembered how the moonlit night captured Donna's high cheekbones and smooth skin. Her honey-fair hair draped over her shoulder, sparkling from the moon's reflection.

Brent cleared his throat. "Are you okay?"

Confliction raged through his body. Donna hadn't texted back. If he told Brent about their fake relationship, then he'd tell Andrea. That could strain the ladies' friendship — he'd never do that to her. Though she'd never come out and directly told him, Donna only seemed to hang out with Andrea, making him wonder why Donna secluded herself.

"My dad laid it on thick last night." Joe shook his head. "Basically, I'm a disappointment because he paid for my degree, and now I'm not using it." Joe cringed. Nothing new — more unmerited criticism from his dad that Joe buried deep, preventing him from lashing out at his dad.

"Did you tell him you designed all the new zip lines, thrill drops, and go-kart tracks?"

"No, Donna did. She let my dad know in no uncertain terms that he was wrong in his thinking."

Brent scoffed, "I get it, so you're mad she made you look like a wuss?"

He didn't get it - not at all. Joe's pride may have been punctured for a mere second. But the persistent feelings of love and appreciation for the woman who spoke highly of him ran deep. His feelings for Donna are real. How would she ever believe that?

"I wish it were that easy." It'd been a long time since he'd told a girl he liked her. He saw the same attraction in her eyes whenever she looked at him, but she always denied it. Was he imagining it?

"I'm confused. You're not mad at your dad for reaming you out again. If it doesn't bother you that Donna stood up for you, what's has your panties in a bunch?"

"Shut it, Betty Crocker." Joe hadn't minded Brent's new-found ability to cook. He'd been the beneficiary of good, home-cooked meals, but one good slam between buddies deserves another.

"Watch it, or you won't get any of the brownies Andrea and I baked last night." Brent side-eyed his friend. "Don't shake your head at me. You can't tell me that you wouldn't do anything Donna asked. At least, I admit that Andrea has me wrapped around her pinky."

As time passed, Joe's mind created a scenario. He would pull Donna out of her seat, press her firmly against his chest, and nuzzle his nose into the softness of her skin. He could already smell her fruity shampoo. Instead of gnawing on her neck like a vampire, he wondered if Donna would prefer him to trail kisses along her slender neck, up to her ear, along her jaw, and capture her full lips.

Joe shook his head, freeing himself of those dangerous thoughts.

Without further ado, Joe blurted out the secret. "Donna and I have been fake dating, but we . . . I broke it off unintentionally before we left Hawaii." Joe blew out a hard breath, deflating all the air from his lungs.

The shock factor on Brent's face burned in Joe's gut, but his shoulders felt a hundred pounds lighter.

"What!?" Brent pulled into the parking lot for the Otter Pond trail — their favorite short hike.

After gathering their packs and securing them on their backs, the guys advanced up the most challenging route. This trail led them around the front, referred to as the mountain's steep side. At not even half the height of Mt. Katahdin, which they'd climbed many times, the summit's route didn't offer much of a challenge. It would still be a good day's outing. Under these beautifully sunny weather conditions, they would be back at the park in five or six hours. Hopefully, by then, Joe could work out his dilemma.

"If you get me in trouble with Andrea . . . Man, this isn't right; I have to tell her." Brent declared, letting go of the branch he'd pushed through. On the return, it slapped Joe in the face. He knew Brent wasn't joking. "This is going to mess up Andrea's plan," Brent slipped.

"What plan?" Joe inquired, reaching for his sunglasses sliding off his head. He secured them over his eyes as the rising sun glanced over the horizon.

Brent let out a sigh. "We're having dinner Friday so that she can explain."

"Tell me now. I shared a huge secret with you. The least you can do is tell me her plan."

Brent's feet skidded to a stop. "*The least I can do*! Really?"

Guilt ate at Joe's marrow, and Brent's glare could have disintegrated him.

"Andrea said that Donna mentioned something in Hawaii about you two not lasting much longer. With you being the best man and her the maid of honor, Andrea thought it would be a good idea — basically, she'd planned on interfering in your life as you and Donna did ours, except now you know about it."

The irony would be laughable if Joe hadn't been so distraught that Donna still hadn't texted him.

"Text Donna again while I grab a drink." He plunked his bag on the trail. "Tell her you need to talk when we return to the park."

"She hasn't even responded to my first text yet. She's at some appointment that she told you about." If Joe's forlorn tone aggravated Brent, he didn't say anything. Instead, he stared at Joe, pointing to his phone.

"Fine." Joe unzipped the pocket on his thigh and pulled out his phone. He typed and erased, typed and erased, and typed and erased again.

Brent grabbed his phone. "Give me that," he said, typing quickly, hitting send, and handing it back to Joe.

Joe read the text. "Sure, make it look easy. You have a woman."

> Donna – we need to talk when I get back to the park. We'll be back around 2. Hope your appointment went well.

They closed their water bottle lids and stored them in their bags. "I get it," Brent began. "it's hard navigating a relationship when you spend most of your time worrying about or wondering what the other person is thinking and feeling. Do you remember what a mess I was with Andrea?"

"Yeah."

"What did you tell me?" Brent urged.

"I can barely remember what I had for breakfast, let alone what I told you months ago."

Brent smirked. "You have it bad."

Joe shoved his friend, who slid on the remnants of mud that the sun hadn't dried yet. "I didn't make fun of you when you fell for Andrea."

"What can I say? You should have fallen first."

Chasing after Brent, Joe stumbled over a tree root, sending him rolling down the trail. A rock stopped him in his tracks.

"That's going to leave a bruise." Joe pressed his palm to his aching ribs and used the rock as leverage to stand up.

"I'm sure Donna can help you with that later," Brent winked at Joe, offering him a helping hand up.

Back at the truck, Joe threw his pack in Brent's backseat. "If Donna doesn't text back, you should tell Andrea so her ideal wedding plans aren't ruined."

"That's not such a bad idea. If you pin yourself down with someone you don't think will ever return your feelings, you're missing out on meeting the one who *will*," Brent's wisdom smacked Joe in the face.

"Right, there could be a woman at the wedding who falls all over me and makes Donna jealous," Joe mused.

"That's not what I said."

"But that's what you meant."

"No. No, it wasn't," Brent shook his head. "That's a great plan, Brent."

At that moment, Joe's phone buzzed with a text from Donna.

Great. I need to talk to you, too.

With eight simple words, hope swelled in Joe's chest. Was it possible he could win Donna over, for real, and didn't need another woman to make her jealous?

<h1 style="text-align:center">Chapter 11</h1>

♥

DONNA'S NERVES THUNDERED THROUGHOUT her body. At five minutes to nine, she pressed the Zoom link the accounting firm in Texas had sent her the previous night. Her interview should go well. She had glowing recommendations. She prayed they wouldn't ask for a recommendation from her current employer since she'd never asked Joe or Brent for one. She listed them as contacts, figuring. She'd have time to explain later.

"Good Morning, Miss Greer. It's a pleasure to meet you. I'm Christopher Smart, the hiring manager for the accounting position, and this is my partner."

"Hi, I'm Darcy Littleton. I'm the direct supervisor for the position you're interviewing for.

"It's a pleasure to meet you both," Donna said a quick prayer, hoping it would calm her nerves.

Donna spent the next fifteen minutes answering their questions and reviewing her resume information, which Donna had submitted electronically to their hiring site.

Donna had relaxed. She preferred account ledgers to zip lines, pencils and pens, to paddles and rackets. She wasn't lazy or out of shape. In fact, she walked, ran, biked, or used the elliptical at least five times a week, so she was physically fit, just not at the same level as Joe and Brent, and no way could she compete with Andrea's upper body strength or her zeal for adventure. The thought soured her mood. It would be hard to leave Andrea, but she had Brent now. Joe wasn't interested in her, but most importantly, her mom needed her help.

"Miss Greer, Did you hear the question?"

Oh, Goodness. Zoning out in the interview is a definite slash against me. Donna chastised herself to stay focused. *Mom is counting on me.* "I'm sorry. Could you repeat it, please?"

"Certainly," his tone didn't show any signs of irritation. "Why didn't you provide any recommendations from your current employers?"

Busted. Just tell the truth.

"They are my friends and don't know about me moving yet. I put them as references, knowing I could break it to them if a prospective employer would be interested in contacting them.

Mr. Smart and Ms. Littleton looked at each other. Donna had the feeling they were conversing in some non-verbal, secret code. Donna's "might be" supervisor took the lead.

"Miss Greer, my team will be better with you if you want the position. As you know from the application, this position will start at the end of summer, the beginning of September. We have a woman leaving upon the birth of her first child."

Elation filled Donna. She never cared about money until she needed *a lot* of it. This job would more than quadruple what she's making from Brent and Joe, allowing her to fulfill responsibilities she'd be taking on.

"I'm going on vacation for three weeks. This gives you some time to have a discussion with your employers. Please let them know to expect my call in about a month."

"Yes, absolutely. Thank you so much for this opportunity."

"We'll be in touch with company paperwork. If you need help finding a place, please let us know how we can help," Mr. Smart offered assistance.

Donna closed her laptop lid. The alert on her phone revealed she only had twenty minutes until she met with Joe. She grabbed her keys and purse and tapped her phone to call her mom, who picked up on the second ring. "Pack your valuables. We're moving to Texas."

She arrived at the park with five minutes to spare. She didn't see Joe or Brent's trucks. *Phew,* Donna let out a breath.

Kevin held the door open for her, and she mouthed, "Thank you," unable to speak aloud since her mom had ranted at her the entire ride.

Closing herself in her office, Donna spoke her piece. "Mom, you need medical attention, or you are going to die."

"I'm going to die anyway, Sweetpea. I don't want treatments."

Tears pooled in Donna's eyes. She bit her bottom lip and held her breath, praying they wouldn't fall. Her mom could always tell when she was crying by her voice.

What is wrong with me? First, Donna's dad had left them before her second birthday. Now, her mom seemed to be giving up on life and Donna.

She felt confused and overwhelmed. She'd interviewed and been offered a fabulous paying job that would potentially save her mom's life. Yes, that job would require them to move to Texas, which would mean leaving her friends behind, but she knew that was the best option for her mother's health.

Then there was Joe. Just mentioning his name broke her fluttering heart. Fake dating had been his idea. Dissolving their relationship, also his idea. Texas might not be far enough away to rid her mind of Joseph Hartley.

"Donna! Are you there?" Her mother blared, demanding her daughter's attention just as the doorknob jiggled.

"Mom, I have to go. We'll talk more about this later." Donna tossed her phone on her desk and fluffed her hair. The least she could do was show Joe what he had given up.

Joe let out a huff of frustration when the doorknob denied him entry. *Why did she lock the door?* He lifted his hand, but it froze in mid-air.

"Knock!" Brent growled behind him.

He pressed down his raging nervous and produced three quick raps on the door. He wiped the sweat forming on his brow. His arms didn't feel comfortable hanging by his side, on his hips, crossed over his chest. *Come on!* He heard footsteps approaching the door, so he grasped the top of the door jamb. When the hollow wooden rectangle swung open, Joe leaned in close enough to catch her fresh springtime air scent, his favorite. She stopped abruptly, almost slamming into his chest. *Shucks.*

Her V-neck shirt showed off her slender neck and collar-bone, both places he'd kissed in his dreams and tortured nightmares.

"Joe." She stumbled back. "I need to change my shirt."

"What's wrong with that one?" *Nothing.*

'I found a stain. You don't want me greeting your guests with a dirty shirt, do you?

With those eyes and lips, perfectly flawless skin, high cheekbones, and immaculately sculpted curves, no one would notice a stain. All it took was talk of a dirty shirt for Joe to fixate on Donna's outward beauty. Why did he torture himself?

'Will you wait for me? I'll be two minutes."

I'd wait forever. "Sure."

He leaned even further forward, tightening his biceps. He refrained from the smirk brewing as Donna's eyes roamed over his arms and chest. "We need to chat, so I'll wait right here."

"Okay. And stop doing that." She waved her finger up and down his arms and torso."

Joe smirked, realizing the effect he had on her.

"Why?"

"Y–you'll break the door jamb." Donna sputtered.

"Right." He took up most of the doorway. Ever so slowly, Joe moved aside, forcing her to twist sideways to pass. Her firm shoulder brushed his chest, causing it to tighten.

She huffed when she stormed by him. He thought he heard her mumble something akin to *stupid muscles.* With a smirk on his face, he watched her sashay away. If he didn't know her better, he'd think she was intentionally torturing him.

A pang of sadness alarmed him. He didn't know much about Donna at all. For the last few months, their conversations had been about scheming and plotting ways for Brent and Andrea to interact. Since Hawaii, today was the first time he'd texted her. At work, they talked about things regarding the park. Hopefully, his plan would work.

He had just settled in her chair when she returned wearing another shirt — this one even more dangerous than the last. The front scooped down, hanging off one shoulder. More skin, really? Where were all those sweatshirts she usually hid herself underneath? Actually, those sweatshirts revealed even more in his imagination.

"What's wrong?" Donna wrapped her arms around her midsection, seeming self-conscious.

Like a pop-up toy, Joe sprang to his feet, a lump clogging in his throat. Her beauty. . .

He forced his voice to work. "Nothing. You're just beautiful." The urge to kiss every pink hue spot in her cheeks overwhelmed his brain.

Donna looked out the door and then shut it with a soft click. "No one is around. I've told you you don't need to waste good comments like that until people are around."

Joe frowned. The hum of the overhead fluorescent lights buzzed in his head. That noise could be mistaken for his growing feelings toward Donna, which he couldn't keep to himself any longer.

"Those words were just for you," his voice low and husky. The words were out of his mouth before he could stop them. Did he regret it? The look of longing on Donna's face answered his question.

His eyes slowly explored the form-fitting shirt that hung past her hips, accentuating all her curves. Then their eyes locked, trying to tell their own story.

Breaking the silence, she exclaimed. "I'm moving away at the end of the summer."

Crickets.

"Joe, did you hear me?"

Another rejection soared through his body. *Loud and clear. So much for the plan. I can't declare my love for her now.* "What brought this on?"

Donna's melancholy demeanor told him that it must be something important. His feet were braver than his heart. He moved in, reaching out his hand, hoping she'd rest her palm in his. Yes. The warmth of her hand pricked his skin, forming goosebumps along his forearm. "If you don't feel like sharing, I understand. I'm a good listener if you need one, though."

"Don't look at me like that," Donna said, snatching back her hand. "You stopped our farce relationship, even though we're still hanging out." She twirled her ponytail around her finger, guarding her abdomen with her other arm. "I can't even deal."

"I plead temporary insanity. You agreed to it, though; what's your excuse?" Joe's voice filled with wonder, no accusation. His heart bled for her.

The rawness deep within his belly couldn't handle seeing tears welling up in Donna's eyes. When a plump tear escaped, flowing down her cheek, Joe couldn't take anymore. He pulled Donna to his chest, letting his shirt absorb her tears. He tried to focus on her pain. Deeming it a challenge wasn't even close. Torture. That was a better description of her warm hands sliding around his lower back.

Leaning down, he whispered in his ear. "What's wrong, Donna?"

"My mom's dying."

Joe's heart skipped a beat. *Oh, crap.* "What can I do?"

"Nothing. She doesn't want—" Donna's phone blared in her pocket, interrupting their moment.

Looking at the screen, she answered instantly. "What's wrong, Mom?"

A strained, petrified look told him something was very wrong. Would Donna tell him?

"I'll be right there." Donna hung up. Grabbing her purse, she avoided looking at him. "I have to go."

"Let me drive you."

"No. I'm good."

Joe didn't have a choice. He had to let her go right now. "Donna—" She stopped briefly, ripping the door open. Her white knuckles gripped the doorknob. "This conversation isn't over. I'll text you later."

She nodded and bolted through the lobby and out the front door. Brent held his hands up, shooting Joe a questioning look, which Joe ignored.

What just happened? He could have sworn Donna had real feelings for him, but then she dropped the bombshell that her mom was dying, and she was leaving. Could he be imagining all this, or was this the worst nightmare he's ever had?

Chapter 12

♥

JOE'S PIERCING BLUE EYES had revealed something she had seen before. Sadness, or was it pity? Her overloaded brain couldn't think straight.

He'd kept his word and texted Donna a few hours after she'd rushed out of her office. When he'd found out neither she nor her mom, Emily, had eaten, he'd brought them her mom's favorite — lasagna from Guido's.

Fortunately, her mom had recovered quickly from her dizzy spell. Her episodes had been increasing, especially after bouts of vomiting. Against Donna's will, her mom had kept telling her that she was nearing the end. How could her mother be okay with leaving her alone? Wasn't that selfish that she'd rather die than seek treatment? Yeah, they would be hard treatments, but wasn't Donna worth it?

Emily wiped her mouth, only able to eat a few bites. She winced in pain, wrapping her arm around her midsection. Joe looked concerned. "Don't fret," Emily began, "I have cancer, so this pain is expected."

Joe's mouth dropped. "I'm so sorry. Had I known, I wouldn't have brought you food you couldn't resist."

Ouch. That felt like a slam. No. Donna hadn't told him until today that her mom was dying of cancer. After all, they were only fake dating.

Emily waved her hand, dismissing his apology. "Thank you, Joe. It's been a long time since I've had anything this delicious. If it's my last meal, it should be my favorite, right?"

"Lovely thought, mother." Donna deadpanned. "Are you sure these doctors know what they are doing?"

"Joe, could you please explain to my daughter that it's my life? I trust the doctors, and if I don't want to endure countless hours of therapy and treatment that will make me feel like crap, that is my prerogative."

Before Joe could speak, Donna rebutted, "Joe, perhaps you could explain to my mother that she has a daughter who'd like more time with her."

"My adult daughter, who should be focusing on getting married, building a family of her own to enjoy."

Solid reasoning, she'd give her mother a point for that, but if her mother thought with her heart instead of her head, maybe she'd get more time with her.

Both women whipped their heads toward Joe, waiting for a response. His mouth hung in an O, and his fork dangled between his thumb and forefinger. He cleared his throat. "I may not have as much common sense as I do book knowledge, but this is one conversation I am staying out of."

Donna bit back a smile. She noticed her mother doing the same. "Sorry. You are right. We can have this conversation another time, where I convince my daughter that moving to Texas, away from Andrea and. . ." Emily's eyes drifted to

Joe, ". . . opportunities right here is stupid. I won't leave my house. I won't put my daughter in a state three times the size of this one to end up completely alone."

Her mother cleared her throat. "Sorry, I'm done now, " she assured her guests.

"We definitely will discuss this later," Donna's passion came from a place of love.

After a performance like that, one would expect awkward silence. Nope. Emily Greer had a mission. Putting Joe and her mother in the same room hadn't seemed like a good idea hours ago. Now, with a devilish gleam in her mother's eye, Donna knew she would regret this.

"So, Joe, what convinced you that fake dating my daughter would be a good idea?"

"Mom!" Donna covered her face with her hands. Her dinner swarmed around her belly like a hive of angry bees ready to attack. How would Joe react? He struggled through a relationship with his disapproving father, and now her mother pounced on him like a hungry tiger.

She wasn't ready for his words. "It was the worst idea of my life."

How could he be so calm about this? Clearly, he didn't want her, but did he have to be so open about it to her mother? Embarrassment enveloped her chest and squeezed like a python crushing its prey.

"Really? Tell me more." Her mother's calm demeanor exasperated Donna. She didn't want to hear the exact details outlining why she wasn't a good fit for the attractive, broad-shouldered, kind man who made her laugh more than anyone ever had.

She already knew. He welcomed every adventure, no matter how big or small. Her? She kicked, screamed, and clawed her way through the last few months. Besides golf and the rock wall, everything else caused her severe anxiety, fright, or physical sickness — very unbecoming.

Her claustrophobic throat prevented any words from escaping. How sad was it that she could have lived the rest of her life in a fake relationship with Joe Hartley? Now that her mother knew the truth — it was the only way to convince her that Texas was a must — she couldn't pretend any longer.

Joe gently gripped Donna's wrists and pulled her hands from her face. He set her hands on her lap without removing his. How was she supposed to concentrate on anything — even if they were words she feared — with his hand like a glove on hers?

For all her days, she would remember that meeting his eyes was the biggest mistake ever. His gaze burned into her retina. Was that a look of longing? No. *He doesn't want you, remember?*

He created this separation, But as the Bible says, everything has its season, and everything happens for a reason. The distance would do both of them good. She needed to guard herself. Regardless of what he said, it was the only way to protect her heart.

Joe gently squeezed her hand. The biceps/tricep action on that side caught her attention. When her eyes met his again, his blue eyes smiled knowingly at her — he'd caught her enjoying his muscles, again. She felt the pressure of a second gentle squeeze, without a doubt looking for the same response. She playfully rolled her eyes. She would have shoved him but didn't want to break their physical connection.

Emily cleared her throat, a reminder they weren't alone, and prompted Joe to answer her question. Hopefully, he remembered it; she couldn't.

"Sorry." Joe ran his free hand through his hair. "I've never been good with girls or women. All my life, they've used me for their purpose and dropped me like a sack of potatoes. From the moment I met Donna, I knew she was special."

If he didn't stop staring at Donna like this, she would do something insane, like kiss him. She couldn't do that. So what if he thought she was special? She wasn't important enough to keep fake dating, and no declaration he made to her mother would matter.

"Yes, she is special, so be mindful of her feelings. Thank you again, Joe, for dinner. I am exhausted and need to get some sleep." She turned to her daughter. "You don't need to stay, I'm fine."

"I'm staying."

"I guess there's no changing your mind. I'll see you tomorrow morning." Emily kissed the top of her daughter's head and left.

Donna began closing the take-out lids, stacking them on each other, and trudging into the kitchen. Joe followed with the trash. He bagged it up. "Do you want me to take this with me?"

"No, that's not necessary," Donna rested the containers between her hand and chin while she used her free hand to open the refrigerator door.

"Here, let me help." Joe dropped the bag and hurried over. She hadn't realized how empty her mom kept her refrigerator. It made sense, though. If she didn't feel like eating, why would she buy food? Donna's heart stung.

Meticulously, Joe grabbed each box, one by one, and put them away. He shut the door but didn't attempt to move. "I know I said I wouldn't get involved, but that was when two women would have torn me apart." Donna chuckled but remained silent. "You're mom made it clear she didn't want to leave her house—"

"Great, you're taking her side. I don't need someone else against me." Donna lit up quickly, like a match to gasoline. She might have tried to keep calm if she had thought for a moment that this was a real relationship. Who was she kidding? When it came to her mother's well-being and her ability to keep her mom here on earth longer, it wouldn't have mattered if her favorite celebrity graced her presence; she would have still exploded.

"Hold up." He grabbed her hand, lacing it with his. "If you were in your mother's shoes, what would you expect from the people around you?"

Not fair. *I don't have children around me.*

"I'll do one better, "What if this were *your* mother?"

"You didn't answer my question, but I'll entertain yours. I don't have a clue what I would do in your situation. I can tell you what I like to *think* I'd do, but that's not reality. This, your situation, is reality."

Good answer. She'd never tell him that. The ticking of her mom's analog clock on the wall — one she refused to get rid of, making sure Donna and her friends knew how to *tell time* — clicked for an undetermined amount of time. Joe hadn't taken his eyes off her the entire time. When the first tear slid from under her eyelash, he pulled her close.

His warm hands on her back felt like a warm blanket from the dyer. Her cheek fit perfectly against his chest. She'd been selfish. All she worried about was her feelings. Her mom had a solid relationship with Jesus, so peace comforted Donna, knowing her mom would meet him, more likely sooner than later. Her pastor told her that moving from one life to the next, when the person is connected with Jesus, isn't hard for the person dying. They are usually excited, or at least embrace the idea of seeing their savior waiting to say, "Welcome home, faithful servant. The left behind are the ones who suffer.

The words hit her like a bungee jumped with a cord too long.

"Shh. It'll be okay. We're here for you." Joe ran his hand down the length of her hair, sending shivers down her spine.

How ridiculous. She was grieving the loss of her mother preemptively, and all her mind could do was focus on the excitement of being this close to Joe.

"I wish you would have told Brent and me about this before you interviewed for a job in Texas. When are you starting?"

"I still need to give them my answer. My supervisor is on vacation for three weeks."

Donna felt Joe's heartbeat pick up pace against her cheek. "What if I asked you to stay?"

Her body stiffened. No. This isn't happening. "Why would you do that?" He didn't owe her anything. Their fake relationship no longer restricted him from living his life. She'd never fit in his world.

"Your friends are here. When your mom does pass on, you're going to need us."

Us? Too bad she didn't want Joe as a friend. Getting distance from the man she'd started falling for was enough reason to leave, even if her mom refused. What would she do if she couldn't change her mom's mind? She'd never leave without her mom. That's not information she'd share with anyone, but it was reality. She would be with her mom as long as possible, wherever that might be.

As usual, God had his plans. Joe pulled her shoulders back slightly and smiled. *Aw, melt my heart.* God never promised an easy life. In fact, He promised trials. Her feet were in the fire, for sure. If she forced her mother to leave — if that were even possible —she'd resent Donna and put a strain on their relationship for the rest of the time her mom had on earth.

"I'd never pressure you into any decision that made you uncomfortable, but your mom made her decision clear. As soon as you tell Andrea and Brent, they will team up against you. . ." his words trailed off for a moment, softening his eyes. "Is there another reason *you* want to leave?"

She squeezed her eyes shut, forcing her mind to focus on anything. Instead, the jumbled mess flinging back and forth from one side of her brain to the other, like the small silver ball in a pinball machine, became blurry.

"I'm sorry, Joe. I can't think straight. I must lie down."

Joe kissed the top of her head. "I understand. Tomorrow is another day; I'll check on you then."

Donna received a text. With his hand on the knob, She grabbed his attention, "Wait, don't go."

He turned, hope in his eyes.

She held up her phone and shook it playfully, "My mom wants to see you alone."

Chapter 13

"OPEN UP!" JOE BANGED on Brent's door. It was only half past nine; his friend was up.

Relief washed over Joe when he saw Brent in the doorway. That relief turned to dread when he noticed Andrea sitting on the couch.

"I need to talk to you alone," he eyed Andrea and then Brent. He paused to see if anyone objected. "I'm sorry, Andrea. It's guy stuff."

"No worries." Sliding to the edge of the couch, she placed her hands on the table before her.

"No, stay. We'll move," Joe assured her.

In the hall, Joe lowered his voice. "Donna's mom wants me to propose to Donna and marry her right away. You know, before Emily dies."

"What?! We have to tell Andrea."

"Tell me what?" Andrea appeared in the doorway. full of guilt, Brent and Joe snapped to attention.

The guys stared at each other. Brent glared at Joe. He should share the information now. "Andrea, you might want to sit for this."

His stomach rebelled, coiling into a ferocious knot. If he thought facing Donna and her terminally ill mom would be a fight, facing off against Andrea was ten times worse. For the next twenty minutes, Joe told Andrea about fake dating, Donna's interview, and a respective job offer in Texas. Her mouth dropped, but it quickly recovered when he revealed her mom's resistance and her desire for Joe and Donna to marry.

After spewing out the details, Joe let out a big huff, collapsing in the nearest chair. Andrea narrowed her gaze at him. He squirmed in his seat like he was back in the principal's office. Thankfully, Brent came to his rescue again.

"Sweetheart, go easy on him. He left out a very important fact."

Joe clutched the arms chairs. *Don't you dare!*

"He has *real* feelings for Donna."

Andrea clapped, "Yay, I can work with this."

Joe leaned forward, resting his elbow on his knees. "Hold up, Andrea. What do you mean? What are you planning?"

He'd seen Andrea's plans in action. He knew this would tick Donna off. Last night, he witnessed her sweet blush when Emily grilled him about his intention. Too quickly, it'd been replaced with sadness, angst, and trepidation about her mother's situation. It might have been wishful thinking on his part, but he thought he also saw a longing in her eyes. Was that desire for him?

His leg bounced nervously, waiting for Andrea to share her plans. "I'm sorry we started this whole mess," he said.

Waving her hand dismissively, "Seriously?" She reached for Brent's forearm, a yearning in their gazes. "Thank you for helping us realize what we wanted before we did."

If they were any more in love, Joe would puke on them. "Get a room," he muttered.

"Touchy, touchy." I plan on fixing this, Joe. Andrea pulled out her phone and texted Donna, he assumed.

Andrea's Joker smile alarmed him. The weight on his shoulder felt more like a boulder, regretting everything he'd done and said the last half hour. "The plan is in motion. Joe, you text Donna and ask her to meet the three of us at Guido's tomorrow at six o'clock. Tell her to bring her mom."

"Who did you just text?"

"Emily Greer." Andrea smiled, pushing off the solid wooden arms on the chair. She hooked her arm around Brent's bicep for support.

"I'll be back once I get Andrea to her car." Brent fist-bumped his buddy. "You've got this."

Joe swallowed the lump in his throat, nerves vibrating through his body. He pulled out his phone, pondering how to say what he wanted. He erased it three times before rereading the final draft and hitting send.

Hey, Donna, I'm thinking of you. Brent and Andrea are going to Guido's at 6 pm tomorrow. I know you don't want to leave your mom alone, so please bring her along.

Normally, he'd glue his eyes on the left side of his phone, anticipating the three waving dots. Right now, his nerves wouldn't let him. Why had Andrea kept him in the dark with her plan?

Not sure how many minutes later, his phone vibrated in his pocket. Tugging it out, Donna's name appeared in the banner on the bottom of his screen, and his face lit up.

He let out a breath when he saw her response.

> Thanks, but I don't think we can make it.

Clearly, she wasn't going to make this easy. "Now what?" He asked aloud.

> Did you ask your mom, or are you answering for her again?

He hit send before he reread it — a big mistake. He knew that even before her response came through.

> Wow! That's none of your business. Remember, *you* let us dissolve.

If he could eliminate that word from the universe, he would. "I miss spoke, Woman. Give a man a break."

> Don't worry about it. I'll invite Emily myself.

Joe quickly texted Andrea, told her what happened, and asked her to text Emily.

You wouldn't dare.

Done.

A few minutes passed before he felt his phone alert him.

You had Andrea text my mom?! What's the deal?

Joe's Insta-smug grin filled his face. He wasn't sure of the plan, but his skin prickled with excitement.

Wipe the smug look off your face, Hartley.

He wasn't sure why that last text made his chest feel like the Mission Impossible match striking a fire within, but she sounded like a girlfriend or wife who knew what her partner was doing without witnessing the action. He wanted that with Donna. If only he hadn't blown it in Hawaii.

According to Andrea's new text, Emily agreed to meet them at Guido's. Maybe Donna wouldn't be upset with him when the information — whatever that is — comes to light. I doubt it.

See you later. *wink emoji*

Donna never responded, which Joe didn't mind. He felt like a kid preparing for a trip to Disney World. Would Donna finally be his?

Chapter 14

J OE CLOSED THE PARK in just enough time. He'd be at Guido's in ten minutes — right on time. A nervous chuckle escaped him as he imagined Donna greeting him at the restaurant. She'd see him approaching the door, and he'd be completely blindsided when she jumped into his arms. "Yeah, right!"

A troubling thought had come to his mind as he traveled along. What if Donna had used him to help Andrea and Brent? The flirty comments she'd kept throwing his way could be a ploy. One to make him think she cared but really didn't.

Guilt suddenly assaulted him. That was not how Donna worked. Besides, his thoughts weren't logical. As Donna had continuously reminded him, it had been his idea to fake date and to break up or dissolve.

He parked his truck right next to Donna's empty SUV. Brent's truck was on the side of the street in one of the handicap spots. Ever since Andrea had had her surgery, she'd wanted to eliminate her handicap placard, but her doctor had refused. She would always need some type of assistance. The walker she'd been using for the last two months was proof of that.

Anxiety filled his full six-three frame. *Breathe, think happy thoughts.* Joe stopped, inhaled through his nose, silently counting to four, and exhaled, counting to four. This usually helped him, but not right now. The unknown was killing him.

The hostess escorted Joe to the back booth, where everyone greeted him. Everyone except Donna. She glared at him. His diaphragm muscle ceased, preventing his lungs from inflating. Was that anger in her eyes, or was it determination? Perhaps it was skepticism. Did she think Joe was responsible for this get-together?

He jerked his chin up, acknowledging her. "Where do you guys want me?"

"Help an old lady up, would you, Joe? Emily stuck her hand out for him to slide her out of the booth. "I'll be back, and I'll sit on the end. That will make it easier for me when I get up again."

He forced his way into the booth, stopping short of his thigh brushing up against Donna's. "Are you okay with this?"

"I have to be, right?" She whispered.

Leaning closer to the side of her head, he offered a genuine solution. "I can move."

Donna tilted her head, closing her eyes. "No, I'm sorry. I feel like you and my mom are up to something, and It's frustrating me."

Great. Watching Donna worry about this while already struggling with her mom's illness was more than heartbreaking. He wouldn't stand by knowing Andrea, with good intentions, he's sure, caused her any more stress.

Emily appeared, ordering Joe around. "Slide in closer to Donna, would you, Son?"

His expanding heart smiled, moving shoulder to shoulder, thigh to thigh with Donna. How long does it take for someone to combust?

"So, Donna," Joe didn't like Andrea's abrupt tone. "When did you plan on telling me about your mom's terminal illness?"

She whipped her head toward Joe, "You told her?" Her accusatory tone shred a hole in Joe's chest. What was she doing?

With a tone only a mom could produce, Emily spoke. "I told her."

Her expression softened. "Sorry." Her eyes shifted from his eyes to his lips, and hers dropped to the table.

I saw that. Did she want him to kiss her? Sandwiched between Donna and her mom was not the time to think about kissing her. Not that it mattered. They'd kiss soon enough at their wedding if Donna said yes.

"Are you moving to Texas to help your mom or get away from Joe?"

Donna huffed out a breath. Not that he was in a rush to hear her answer, Joe noted that she hadn't responded. Was all this his fault? First, he'd messed up his dad's dreams of having a son work by his side; now, he chased Donna away.

If he'd learned to stand up and speak freely at an early age, he wouldn't have caused so much destruction as an adult.

Silence fell over the table like a black storm cloud. Saved by the waitress. We ordered. When the waitress left, a more awkward silence filled the booth.

"So, this is what the young people do nowadays. In my day, we spoke to one another." Emily's matter-of-fact tone made Joe chuckle.

"Please tell me you plan on staying around for our wedding," Andrea reached for Donna's hand across the table.

"Of course, I wouldn't miss it."

Andrea clapped her hands together. "Emily, it would be an honor if you'd stand in as the bride's mother." Andrea didn't have to say how hard it would be getting married without her parents. They'd died in a car accident — the same one that permanently injured Andrea.

With glassy eyes, Emily reached for Andrea's hand. "It would be my pleasure. I don't think I'll get this job before I die unless, of course, Joe decides to marry my baby any time soon."

Joe sprayed soda from his mouth, dousing the table with a syrupy liquid.

"I'd take that as his answer, Mom. Go with Andrea. She's a sure thing." Donna's dejected voice made Joe's heart twinge.

Andrea glared at him.

He shrugged. *You could warn a man.* She knew women intimated him. He'd told Andrea about Kara dumping him when he stopped writing her business plans and giving her stock market tips.

Now, he had a woman who was just the opposite. Donna comforted and assured him, but wasn't that all pretend? Somehow, he doubted it, but since he'd pushed her away, it felt awkward to ask.

"Mom, are you sure you're up for the trip? They are doing a destination wedding."

She chuckled. "This coming from the girl who wants to trek me almost two thousand miles away from my home."

Emily had yet to eat much off her plate. Joe wondered how long it'd been since she'd lost her appetite. Though she didn't look frail, he knew it wouldn't be long if she didn't get more nutrition.

"I didn't tell anyone, but the doctor told me I only have weeks left, not months."

"WHAT!?" Donna shook her head. "Something isn't right. I know cancer can happen to anyone, but there was literally nothing wrong with you at your physical three months ago, yet now you have the number one type of lethal cancer." Donna's fingers strummed the table. "Even if you don't want to move to Texas, let's go see if. . ." her words trailed off. "There's something fishy about this. I can feel it."

A dreary silence fell over the table. Joe pushed his plate away. Donna had barely touched hers anyway. Joe couldn't imagine how she felt.

"This is why I don't want to go to Texas. I'll die before you know it, and then you'll be down there without these very important people in your life," Emily motioned toward Joe,

Brent, and Andrea. "You need to call that accounting firm and tell them you're not moving to Texas. You've made it clear that you won't be leaving the house, so you should give up your apartment and move back into your old bedroom. Once I die, you'll have a house to start building your family." She winked at Donna and Joe.

"Yeah, about that. . ." Donna began.

Fearing Donna was about to say something that would reveal he'd shared their secret with Brent and Andrea, Joe quickly slipped his hand in Donna's, squeezed it, and smiled. "We haven't talked about marriage, but I'd marry her today If she'd let me."

Drink malfunction number two of the evening: Donna began to spit and sputter like a gas tank full of water. Joe knew she wasn't choking, so he gently drew circles on her back with his palm, hoping to comfort her until the coughing fit subsided.

"Excuse me. I need to use the restroom." Donna nearly shoved Joe out of the booth once her mom stood.

He wondered if Andrea should have gone with her. He seriously wondered if Donna would return.

Emily smiled. "Are you ready for this?" She handed him a maroon-colored velvet box. "You promise me that you have real feelings for my baby and won't drop her once I'm dead?"

"I'm in love with your daughter," Joe delivered without hesitating.

Emily waved him off. "Be serious. She'll be back any minute. You make my daughter happy, and you have superb character references." Brent and Andrea grinned at him. "You ask her to marry you, then we stay here; she works for you, and you give her babies to raise. She'll be a great mom.

Joe opened the box. "Oh, wow!"

Emily smiled. "It was mine. She always talked about having it. I never thought it would be possible, yet here we are." her downtrodden tone made him frown.

Emily placed a hand on Joe's forearm. "If you don't want to marry Donna, then I won't pressure you, but I can see it in Donna's face and hear it in her voice; she loves you. Unless I'm terrible at reading people, you love her as well." She wiped a tear from her cheek. "I'd love to see my baby girl walk down the aisle with a kind man like you. One that would love her the way she needs to be loved."

Oh, boy. Talk about a punch to the gut. He couldn't take that joy away from Emily. She was right. He did have strong feelings for Donna, and marrying her would give him more time to fall in love.

"Is the plan clear enough?" Brent mocked him.

Realizing this would be the easiest and hardest thing he's ever done, Joe pocketed the ring and agreed, "Okay, I'll do it."

"Do what?" Donna asked, arriving from the backside of the booth.

Chapter 15

Sleep deprivation prevented Donna from making rational decisions, so she was thankful when Brent told her she could work from home indefinitely. He'd agreed to drop off a few things from her office later that evening.

It had been two days since their outing at Guido's, and Emily had grown weaker. Unsteady on her feet, she'd been bedridden.

"I need a new change of scenery," Emily begged.

Donna was strong and her mom small, but the daunting task of picking up her mom loomed over her. Hearing her mom groan in pain with every shuffle toward the living room severed Donna's heart.

"Let me get you a wheelchair."

"No, I can do it," Emily insisted.

Donna shook her head at her mother's stubbornness. "Your doctor said if you had had even one treatment, you wouldn't be in such pain now."

"He doesn't know. He's not God."

True. Her mother did have a way of revealing the truth.

"Spending your last days in pain is asinine," Donna all but yelled.

Emily's weak voice. "It's my decision."

They finally reached the couch. Donna helped her mom lay down and then sat at the end of the couch by her mom's feet.

The deafening silence put Donna's brain on overtime. She'd given up the idea of moving her mother to Texas, but couldn't she go? Staying here wasn't feasible. The accounting firms were a joke, speaking specifically about compensation. Donna had never been hung up on money. Heck, she'd packed her entire apartment and brought the boxes to her mom's. She didn't need material things to satisfy her existence.

Based solely on principle, working equally as hard or harder than an accountant in Texas, yet receiving less pay, didn't make sense.

Her mom had already started talking about the morbid side of her illness. Donna had never thought she'd be having this conversation with anyone in her twenties, let alone her mom — her rock.

"I have three more payments on the house. The severance package I got from the insurance company will cover that. I also have some credit card bills that I'll pay off this month. Then it's all yours. Use it to buy food for us, whatever comes up." Mom didn't live frivolously, either. Thank God. Donna couldn't imagine being weighed down with debt and losing her mom.

"I have a hundred thousand dollar life insurance policy I purchased on my own. It's in a box at the foot of my bed." Mom had always been organized, but she'd never kept a box at the end of her bed. "I also have one from work. That's a bit higher because they contributed."

Oh, Lord, please let her stay here with me for as long as possible, but don't let her suffer.

Talk about a double-sided request. She was in pain right now, but Donna couldn't imagine her mom dying today.

On cue, Emily winced in pain, grabbing her midsection. Liver cancer and pancreatic cancer at the same time. Really? Alone, each was a death sentence. Obviously, together, it meant a shorter death sentence. How long had her mom been pushing through the pain so she didn't alarm Donna? The potential answer crushed her.

"What can I get you, Mom?"

Emily waved her hand dismissively, but Donna ignored the sentiment. Still not sure what would actually help her, Donna got her mom a blanket and covered her from the tips of her toes to underneath her chin.

For the remainder of the day, Donna held her mom's hand and talked, putting a moratorium on the life-after-death discussion. At about one o'clock, she forced a protein shake into her mom.

"Tell me about Joe," Emily requested.

Donna shrugged. "I don't have much to tell that you don't already know."

"Sure you do. I'd like to hear about how you two fell in love."

Donna choked on her thick shake. "Mom, we were fake dating, you know that."

"I must have forgotten with all the steamy looks you shot each other the other night."

In the future, Donna would have to be careful. Playing along for her friends is one thing, but she couldn't risk revealing her feelings. She'd never want Joe to feel bad that he didn't have feelings for her.

Like she could read Donna's mind, her mom said, "Honey, the man has feelings for you. Don't push him away."

Feeling vulnerable, Donna shook her head. "Nah. He couldn't even handle fake dating. Joe refused to admit that it even happened. He rather we dissolve—"

"Enough with that excuse." Shocked into silence, Donna waited for her mom to finish. "Have you considered he gave that as an option because he didn't know how you were feeling?"

Consider that? She'd spent most nights praying and hoping that had been the case. Too bad her scaredy-cat tendencies ran deep. She'd never ask him, fearing the answer. Of course, he wouldn't build a lifetime around her. Joe spent his life outside on adventures; Donna had tagged along to make the relationship believable.

Liar! Donna had started to enjoy the adventures. Though her stomach revolted against most of the time, her heart enjoyed spending time with Joe.

"The look on your face right now tells me everything I need to know. Relationships involve risks. I knew your dad was the biggest gamble, but I took it, and I don't regret a second of my time with him."

Donna didn't understand that nonsense. Chad Greer worked her mom over. He convinced her that he could settle down, and they married. Donna, a honeymoon baby, arrived too soon for her dad's liking. Emily always defended him.

"You need someone who loves you." Emily reached for her daughter's hand. "Donna, we've been looking out for each other for so long," she sighed, "when a man loves you and looks out for you, it's a feeling like no other."

Her animosity toward her dad resurfaced when she saw the longing look on her mom's face. If she ever saw that man, *ugh!* Another harsh reality hit her. She wouldn't know it if he stood right next to her.

"The only thing I know about him is that he likes to put his life on the line daily. He has an engineering degree, a sweet mom, and a tyrant dad."

"That's a start."

"He knows even less about me."

"Now, there's a surprise,"

"Sarcasm gets you nowhere. Isn't that what you've always told me?"

"You never listened." Emily shrugged. "Turns out you were right; sarcasm is amusing to use."

Donna rolled her eyes.

Reaching for and grabbing Donna's hand, Emily pleaded, "Try again. Joe is a good man. If he tries to explain himself, hear him out. I believe he loves you."

A pregnant pause filled the room.

"As a matter of fact, you two should do the love language quiz."

"What?"

"Oh, girl, you haven't heard of it?"

"Of course I have, Mom. I'm shocked that you have."

"It's hard to love someone else unless you love yourself. I did this when I met your dad. We shared our love language and then used it to show our love for each other."

"That worked out well." More sarcasm.

"Joe isn't your dad. Besides, I learned even more the second time I took the test — two days after your dad left. I needed to make sure I could be the best mom for you. I had to love myself first."

"Hmmm. So I'm hearing that I should just take the test to find out how I can love myself because Joe's already made it clear that we are not a couple, not even a fake one."

"Get the cobwebs out of your ears, girl." Emily rattled her daughter's hands. "Call it mother's intuition, but Joe likes you. If you do this together, you will learn how to love one another and have a happy life."

"Earth to Mom, return from your sappy romance novel or ridiculous Disney princess movie. That sounds even more fake than our dating. If he knows the exact way I need to be loved and just does it, how long before he gets tired of doing it and leaves like your husband did?" Donna hated calling him Dad.

"When we know better, we do better. Again, Joe is not your dad. I see it in his eyes."

Donna twirled her ponytail around her finger — wound it tight, and released. What if her mom was right? She could be missing out on love. But, if her mom was wrong, she'd be in more pain when he left her.

The doorbell pulled her from her pity party thoughts. Looking at her smartwatch, Donna freaked. "Mom, it's five o'clock. Where did the day go? This must be Brent, but I'll get you dinner afterward."

"Okay, dear."

That was too easy. Her mom had fought a protein shake at lunch. When Donna reached the door, she plastered her best smile and pulled it open, expecting Brent.

Instead, Joe, Andrea, and Brent greeted her. Joe looked sick — sweat forming at his hairline and blanched cheeks. "We brought dinner," Andrea exclaimed. She'd been more cheery since she and Brent got engaged, but Donna's suspicion rose.

"Here are all your folders," Brent said, handing them over. Donna slowly reached for them like they were protected by an electric fence, ready to shock her at any moment.

"T-thank you. It took all three of you to bring me this?" Donna questioned.

Andrea laughed it off. "Gosh, no. We brought dinner."

"That's sweet, thank you," Emily sat up straighter.

Joe held a baking dish between two potholders. "Can I put this in the kitchen?"

"Yes, please. Donna, go help him."

Help him. . . with what? Donna pushed the swinging door forward, thinking Joe would enter, but he didn't.

"You go first."

Oh, man! His smile is lethal.

She held the door for him once he was in the kitchen. He brushed his shoulder against hers as he approached the counter. If that wasn't enough, he winked at her. *What the heck?*

Donna released the door, letting it slowly swing until it stopped altogether. She questioned Joe's actions with her arms crossed over her chest and an edge of frustration on her tongue. "What was that wink for?"

Turning around, Joe flashed her a smug grin, leaned back on the counter, and mimicked Donna's arm position.

Not fair! Donna's eyes slowly roamed over Joe's upper body. Joe's biceps begged his shirt to free them. When her eyes reached his, he didn't waste any time teasing her. "You like what you see?"

Yes! "You wish. I wondered why you're winking at me and mocking my stance?"

"You're feisty tonight," Pushing off the counter, Joe closed the gap between them. "I like it."

Hmmm. With Joe so close, all Donna could focus on was his cedar wood scent with a faint jasmine to compliment the manly fragrance.

"Where are the plates beautiful?"

Donna pointed to the cupboard to her right. "Ugh. Stop sending me mixed messages."

Watching Joe plate out the chicken, rice, and broccoli made her heart flutter. Instantly, Donna began wondering what it would be like to cook with or for Joe every night. This domestic thought made her breath hitch as she watched his triceps flex as he stretched his arm to the plate furthest away.

"Are you looking at my butt?" Joe teased.

"No, definitely not." Ah, the truth — what a relief.

Joe peeked over his shoulder. "So you're checking out my muscles then."

"What? No." Heat flooded her face — stupid light complexion.

He smirked and finished plating the food.

"Seriously, Joe, why are you playing games with me?" She sounded like a needy girlfriend — *perhaps that's why he doesn't take you seriously.*

With arguably the most sexy look on his face, Joe pinned her against the counter with a hand on each side of the granite surface waist level. She sucked in a breath. At this range, she saw his tight jaw. It's a wonder he hasn't busted any teeth clenching so hard.

"I've misspoken and haven't been brave enough to say things, but I've never, nor would I ever, play games with you. To clear things up. I will do whatever it takes for you to fall in love with me."

Hello, brain, are you there? Aren't you in charge of telling my lungs to breathe?

Slowly, as if his words hadn't tortured her enough, he leaned in, his trim beard tickling her cheek, and whispered, "Clear enough?"

Still unable to talk but fortunately back to breathing, Donna shook her head.

"Perfect, grab a couple of plates and help me carry them out."

Dinner seemed tense as if everyone around her knew something she didn't.

"He Dear, can you get me my blanket from my bed? Halfway toward the hall, she turned back, and the words meant for her mom lodged in her throat when Joe appeared in front of her on a bent knee. Her mouth fell open, but she quickly recovered it. The corners of his mouth quirked up. The only noise in the room was her erratically beating heart.

He gripped her freezing hand — all of the blood drained from her limbs — and squeezed it gently. Tears filled her eyes. *Seriously, what are you crying for? He's mocking you!*

Her stomach tightened. This couldn't be happening. *What was his angle?* Joe had never lied to her but skipped some crucial details. Her mom smiled like the cat that ate the canary — clearly, she knew about this proposal. Based on the goofy looks on Andrea and Brent's faces, they knew, too.

"Donna, I know it hasn't been quite a year. . ." she surveyed his eyes as he spoke, hoping he'd reveal a hint of why he was proposing right now. Instead of answers, his dark pupils flared at her, causing her stomach to do a backflip. ". . . but I'm ready to start my life, and I'd like you to be my wife."

She tilted her head, *That's your proposal?* Off to the side, Brent slapped his head against his forehead.

Emily encouraged her daughter. "Don't overthink it, dear. Joe's a good guy,"

He gave her a cute, half smile. "I'll do everything in my power to make you happy," Joe insisted. Her heart dared to hope — Joe might have real feelings for her. Another doubt wormed its way into her thoughts. Even if he did have feelings, how long would they last before he left her, too?

Her breath quickened. Donna agreed, "Yes, I'll marry you." Joe slid the ring, her mom's ring, on her finger. Pushing to his feet, he embraced her. His strong arms wrapped around her felt like an electric blanket in the middle of June. "I don't know what you're up to, but I will find out," she whispered in his ear.

Chapter 16

♥

"WHAT AM I GOING to do?" Joe yelled into the phone. "Donna will be here any minute."

Joe frantically picked up and zoomed around his apartment, tidying it up. Last night, he'd asked her to marry him. What had he been thinking about springing it on her like that?

Brent chuckled, too amused at Joe's emergency. "Tell her the truth."

"Which one?" Joe felt like a heel. This all started when he wasn't straight with Donna about finding her attractive almost a year ago. Instead, he let the fear from his thirteen-year-old self emerge. Too many times, girls used him to get good grades but then went on to date a more popular guy. That he could understand. The times it really bothered him were when they moved on with someone Joe deemed less attractive than him or just a plain jerk.

"Oh, what tangled web we weave—"

"Shut it! This all started because you and Andrea had issues, and we were trying to help, so don't act like Mr. Perfect."

Brent sighed. "If I have the complete story, this is an easy solution. Tell her you never wanted to fake date but were too scared to put yourself out there. You got scared she would leave you, so you broke it off in Hawaii. You realized your mistake; you love and want to marry her."

"It's not that easy," Joe grumbled. "She took another job out of state to get away from me."

What had he been thinking? There was no way Donna was ever going to fall for him. He was collateral damage to every other girl he'd dated. *Oh, Joe, can you please help me with my physics paper? Joe, sweetheart, can you help me study for the trig test?* Did those girls know they didn't have to sweet-talk him? Joe prided himself on helping anyone who asked.

Those girls flirted and insinuated relationships with them, but, like his dad, they only wanted a relationship with Joe if he could offer them something.

The faint sound of a door slamming grabbed his attention. Pulling back the curtain, he saw her car. "Great, she's here."

"You've got this. Bye, buddy." Brent hung up.

Joe pulled the phone from his ear and stared at it, half wishing Brent's voice would come back and say something to assure him, while the other half wished he could crawl through the phone and choke Brent. He wouldn't be in this predicament now if he'd never told Brent about the fake dating.

A soft knock on his door. Joe blew out a breath and pocketed his phone. He straightened his spine and squared his shoulders. Even if he didn't feel confident, he'd fake it. Frustration burned his insides. The idea of faking something else caused his shoulders to slump a little as he gripped the door. He ran his fingers through his tousled hair and flung open the door.

"Hey." He leaned against the door, trying to look casual and relaxed. Joe swept his arm toward the living room with an open, flat palm, welcoming her into his space.

His expression dulled when she scowled at him after stepping in a few feet and stopping. Joe hung his head as he gently shut the door. *Lord, please give me the words that I need to make this better.*

Forcing a smile on his face, Joe turned. Their nearness kicked his heart up a notch. He stuffed his hands in his pocket and took a step back. *Please don't say anything stupid.* Joe's insides threatened to appear on the floor.

He sighed, "Go ahead, give it to me."

Donna's foot turned out, and her hip jutted in the opposite direction. "Please correct me if my timeline is off."

Her calm voice sent firehouse alarms off in his head.

She began ticking items off on her fingers. "I asked for your help so Andrea didn't kill herself on Katahdin. You suggested we fake date since it would force Brent and Andrea together." She pressed her third finger back, stating, "Instead of us telling them the truth and getting a great laugh about this, you just want to pretend I never existed. I told you I was moving out of state, and now you've asked me to be your wife. Does that about cover it?"

"Sounds about right," Joe agreed.

She crossed one leg over the other. "Great, now tell me why."

Her demanding voice surprised him. Where did his sweet Donna go? Before he could answer, she continued.

"We both know that you do not love me. I will not marry anyone who doesn't love me. . . for any reason. I refused to end up like my mom."

Joe raised his eyebrows, wondering what she meant by that, but judging by the wave of her dismissive hand, now was not the time to ask.

"Do you love me?" He wasn't sure he wanted to know the answer. He wouldn't be surprised if she said no, but it might crush him.

A pregnant pause filled the room. She twirled her ponytail three times. "I never thought about it since this was all fake."

Not exactly what he wanted to hear, but it wasn't the outright rejection he'd received from past females or his dad.

"I need to know what has changed for you." She held up her digits and wiggled the engagement ring Joe had placed on her hand last night.

At the same time, he felt his bravery slip away. Emily's words, *Tell her I want to see her get married before I die,"* filled his mind. Would she go along with the marriage if it made her mother happy?

Joe snuck a glance at her scrunched–up face. Even frustrated, this woman had desire churning in his gut. Donna was crazy beautiful and a major distraction.

"Your mom mentioned wanting to see us get married before. . . you know." Joe couldn't bring himself to voice her mom's inevitable destiny.

She facepalmed herself. "We can't just get married because my mom wants that."

"You've always seemed off when it came to marriage; how come?" Joe hoped he sounded as sincere as he meant it. He motioned for her to take a seat on the couch.

He fought the urge to sit next to her. Instead, Joe sat with his back to the couch arm, crooked his elbow on the high back, and rested his head in his palm.

Big mistake. Her profile was just as heart-stopping beautiful as the frontal view.

"Does it have anything to do with why you don't have a sense of adventure?"

She scoffed. "Just because I don't find it fun to dangle my body fifty feet above the ground with jagged rocks protruding out that would inevitably slice me to shreds on the way down as you do doesn't mean I don't have a sense of adventure. I agreed to fake date you, didn't I?"

Now, he understood her hesitancy in marrying him. "Ah, I see. I'm not good enough. I get it."

She reached out her hand and rested her palm on his forearm. As she gripped his muscles tightly with her slender fingers, they stiffened under her grasp, causing him to clench his jaw. *Please don't let me bust any teeth, Lord.* Donna dipped her chin in an attempt to capture his eyes. "I was just kidding."

"Yeah, it's no big deal." He'd never been good enough to date. Like his dad, people valued him only if he could do something for them. Sadness clutched his chest.

"Do you think I was serious because of how your dad treats you?" She wasn't going to let this go, was she?

Joe shrugged. "It would be difficult to deny that after you witnessed his behavior." Her fingers began to caress his arm, and she inched closer. His heart sped up.

"Joe, don't let your dad dictate your decisions in life." The room stilled.

Why was she smirking after giving such sound advice? Was *the prospect of marrying me that bad?*

"Will you stay for dinner?"

"Yeah, okay."

They worked together in the small kitchen. Joe imagined cooking dinner with Donna every night and envisioned more touching and fooling around. She is technically his fiancé. He could press his luck now, couldn't he?

"It's not just my dad. All through school, girls used me to get good grades." Her eyes grew wide. "They didn't use me that way." He gently flicked the dishtowel at her hip. "Looking back, they never really promised anything; they just flirted and acted like they were interested in me, but once they got what they wanted, they were off to date the guy they really wanted.

"Oh, Joe. That's horrible. Who does that?"

He shrugged. "I think it happens more often than not. That's why it meant the world to me when you stood up to my father."

"It was nothing."

"No one has ever done that for me before." Their gazes locked. Her eyes were telling him to kiss her. If she were his wife, he'd grip her hips and pull her close to his chest. Then he'd kiss her soundly until the food burned and then kiss her some more.

Stop. This wasn't easy for Joe. Being around Donna was sweet torture. If he didn't focus, he would burn their food, but he wouldn't have the pleasurable kiss, making it okay. "I think the burgers are done," he burst out, rushing back to the stove.

What would it take to convince her to marry him? He was playing for keeps, but if it was fake to her, would it ever be real in her mind?

Joe pulled out the condiments. Their fingers brushed against each other when he handed her the pickle jar.

"Who eats pickles on their burger?" Donna sounded insulted, but her smirk told him otherwise.

"Anyone who eats at a fast food joint."

She scoffed. "Who eats at those? You're way too fit to eat at a place like that."

"Thank you for the compliment. You are correct," Joe winked.

"About what? That you're fit or don't eat artery-clogging food?"

Joe smirked. "Both, but definitely the being hot and muscular part."

Donna tipped her head back and roared. "I didn't use those words."

But you wanted to."

"You keep telling yourself that."

During dinner, Joe got Donna to open up about her dad. It nearly ripped Joe's heart out. He couldn't stand guys who left their families.

That might explain her feelings about marriage. Was she afraid that Joe would leave her? What damage had Joe already done in Hawaii? He had such a big mouth.

She licked ketchup off the corner of her mouth. His throat clogged.

Stop staring. Look away.

She put her burger down and dabbed the remaining red sauce with a napkin. The urge to clean it off with a kiss overwhelmed him.

"Want some?" She teased.

Could she read his mind or what?

"Is that a legitimate offer?"

She put the napkin back on her lap.

Guess not. Disappointment ran wild through his gut.

After insisting on helping clean up, Donna thanked him for dinner. He couldn't let her leave yet. "Um, shouldn't we finalize the plans?" Their proximity had his senses soaring.

Donna's skeptical look dampened Joe's happiness. That look told him that even Donna knew he wasn't worthy. She was just a nice, sweet person who would stand up for someone, but that didn't mean she wanted to marry him. It was time for him to get real, or he could lose her forever.

What's your plan? Are we going to divorce when my mom dies?" Before he could answer, she continued. "I mean, it's really sweet of you to think about my mom's feelings, but isn't marrying me a bit much?"

"It's a dream come true." His voice escaped huskily. Her expression softened.

Did he believe her?

Chapter 17

♥

EMILY WOKE UP FEELING stronger the following day. Donna found her in the kitchen making eggs.

"Do my eyes deceive me, or are you feeling better? How?" Donna asked, her voice filled with relief.

"I called the doctor's office while you were gone last night. Dr. Campbell was on call and made a house call."

"Okay," Donna cautiously walked toward her mom, her concern palpable. "Everything alright?"

"Yup. Gave me some pain medication that will 'help me function,'" she spoke in a deep baritone voice to mimic her doctor. "He told me it will work until it doesn't."

It was still a mystery to them how Emily got sick. Dr. Campbell was new to the practice when he saw Emily for her checkup, which was another reason why Donna wanted her mom to get a second option at the cancer center. They didn't know this new doctor. She was happy her mom wasn't in pain, but a doctor making a house call nowadays seemed fishy.

Donna hugged her mom from behind. "I'm glad you're not in pain. That was killing me.

"I've got to see my baby walk down the aisle."

Then, the ambush began.

"How'd your night go? When are you guys getting married? We should figure it all out because I don't have any more time, just less pain while I'm here."

Please, don't remind me.

"Funny you should ask." Donna rubbed her temples in a circular motion. "Joe doesn't love me. Do you know why a man who doesn't love me would ask me to marry him using your ring nonetheless?"

Her mother turned her attention back to the stove where she had eggs and home fries sizzling. "Please don't be foolish, my love. That man loves you."

She wouldn't fight with her mother since she only had a short time left. She wondered why her mother wanted her to turn out like her. Wasn't she unhappy? She'd fallen in love. He'd lied, saying he'd love her to the end, but he'd left her with a toddler instead.

"Are you happy, Donna?" Her mother probed.

"At the moment, I'm confused and frustrated," her tone irritated.

The corner of Emily's mouth lifted slightly. *Glad she can find amusement in my stress.* If she hadn't made such a fuss about moving or getting treatment, this would have been a moot point and would have alleviated most of Donna's concerns.

"Were you happy when you were *fake dating?*" Her mother whispered the last two words as if the FBI had bugged the house.

"I was less stressed, yes."

"You and Joe are meant to be together. My marrow tells me so." Emily turned around, pointing a spatula at her daughter, "No cracks about my marrow being bad."

Donna huffed. "First of all, that's not funny under any circumstance, and secondly, that's not even the type of cancer you have unless you're keeping something from me."

"I'm just trying to lighten you up. You act like I'm going to die any second. The doctors said—"

Donna cut her mother off abruptly. "Doctors and God don't always work on the same timetable." Her mother's lack of concern for herself bothered Donna. She had even asked a lawyer if she could force her mother to be seen by a psychologist and declared unable to make her own decisions. Then Donna could force the treatments.

In the end, it would have been a long road to prove that she was mentally incapable. It's funny that people can choose to die instead of getting better even when they have children. The lawyer pointed out that Donna was almost thirty years old. Rationally, she understood and never pursued it. Still, all she heard and saw was her mother withering away of her own accord, leaving Donna behind, eventually, just like everyone else in her life did.

Joe was trying to get back into her life, but something seemed awry with the marriage proposal. Was Joe marrying her because he wanted to, or had her mom coerced him? How selfish. She was choosing to die, yet she tried to control Donna's life beforehand.

Maybe she should go back to bed. This day wasn't starting well. "You're heading into the office today," her mother announced matter-of-factly.

"Excuse me?"

"I want to get out. It's a good day. This will give you a chance to be among the living."

"You're still alive, Mom." Donna plopped in a chair, feeling discouraged.

"That's not what I meant, and you know it."

She did need to talk with Joe. If he genuinely meant marrying her would be a dream come true, they might have a chance. She already knew how she felt; all that remained was getting the truth from him.

"Why haven't you dated much?" Emily plated the food and handed one to Donna.

"What's the point? Dad left after promising to stay." Her body was filled with regret and sadness.

"And Rick still left for New York even though he said he'd stay here with you."

Tears pooled in her eyes. "Everyone leaves me. . . on purpose. Now you are, too."

Emily placed her plate on the table and pulled Donna to her feet. "Aw, Baby. Your dad left me. He couldn't take being tied down to one person, job, or mundane life. Mark didn't leave you. He left for a shot at life. You may have left him once you were in the Big Apple. You two were not meant to be. Now Joe—"

Donna choked on her tears. "Oh, Mom." She sniffed. "Do you think Joe is being sincere?"

She shook her head. "I know you've seen the man look at you. Stop ignoring the signs. Now eat so we can go, and you can officially accept that proposal."

They never made it to the office. Once they finished cleaning up, Andrea called and suggested they go dress shopping. Donna hadn't seen her mom jump up and down in a long time, and the action warmed her heart. She'd do anything to make her last days as enjoyable as possible.

When they reached the bridal store, Andrea already had the saleswoman hopping. At least ten dresses were hung on a silver roll cart next to a dressing room, and her name was plastered on the front in black letters.

"Hey, girlie, we're here." Donna skimmed through the dress options, fingering the material. The silky ones would be her choice, but she was here to support Andrea. She shouldn't be thinking about what she'd wear to her wedding. She hadn't even accepted his proposal yet.

"Aren't they beautiful?" Andrea queried.

"Yeah, but they don't remind me of you?"

Andrea shook her head. "Of course not, silly, these are for you."

"Me?" Shock flooded her face.

"You're going to need one before me," Andrea said matter of factly.

What would make her think that? Her eyes narrowed in on her friend's face. "What do you know that I don't?"

"Brent said you and Joe talked . . . I'm going to kill him. I never should have relied on Brent to give me accurate information."

Donna rolled her eyes. Still unsure of what she was missing, it bothered her that her mother and Andrea seemed to *see it*. What was going on? Was she so closed off that with Joe giving mixed signals, she'd only paid attention to the heart-wrenching comments about them dissolving?

"He loves you, Donna." Andrea's tone was soft and tender.

Emily rubbed her hands together. "Go try these on, Donna. I can't wait to see you in them."

For the next three hours, Donna tried on every dress Andrea picked out and even a couple more that her mom had snuck on the rack while Donna was changing. The excitement started filling her soul. If Joe had developed an attraction to her as she had him, would that be enough to build a real marriage? Was it possible that she was going along with someone else's plans like she always did?

The final dress. Donna lost her runway walk and modeling technique over an hour ago. She finally put her foot down and took the petticoat off. This halter top–styled dress with sequins from the straps through the bodice complimented her. The silky feel of the bottom half of the dress felt better on her bare legs than the itchy petticoat.

"How do you know?" Donna narrowed her eyes at Andrea as she exited the dressing room.

"What?"

"That Joe has real feelings for me."

"Where I come from, any man who puts your safety as a top priority is in love. Speaking from experience and all." Andrea winked at her, referring to how she and Brent met. Andrea had despised him for putting her safety first. At the time, she hadn't zip-lined since developing paraplegia, and he didn't want her to get hurt or injure any of his employees. Andrea clearly loved Brent now. Had she been willing to see Brent for the man he was from the beginning, Donna and Joe wouldn't be in this mess now.

Andrea continued, "Joe is Mr. Adventure. He went with you on all the beginner excursions to ensure you were comfortable. Joe was there when you landed after your first skydiving experience—"

"—First and last."

"Donna, he loves you. It doesn't mean he doesn't feel it if he hasn't said it yet. Guys are dumb; they don't share their feelings. Oh, wait, neither do you. Houston, I found the problem." Andrea changed the famous quote to prove her point."

She was right. It was time for Donna to be honest about whether she would take control of her life. "Could we have a few minutes?" Donna asked Ari, the saleswoman.

The young woman excused herself and promised to return in a few moments. Her mom was already looking at more dresses.

"Andrea, I've been keeping something from you."

"What is it? Andrea moved her walker to the side so Donna could sit beside her.

Donna blew out a breath. She twirled the ring Joe had placed on her finger. "Right before your accident, I received a job offer in New York City just like Mark. I turned it down to stay here with you. I didn't want you to be alone. Recently, I've started wondering, what if? So when I found out about Mom, that's why I searched for the best treatment hospital for her and applied for a new job."

Andrea's shocked expression worried Donna. Was she mad at her for not taking the job? She couldn't be mad that she'd stayed to help her, could she?

"You don't need me anymore now that you have Brent. I figured it was time to make a change."

Fast as lightning, Andrea pulled Donna in for a hug. "That is the most absurd thing I've ever heard. I'll always need you. You're my best friend," she spoke in Donna's ear. They separated. "Are you saying you continued to work as an office secretary until we met Joe and Brent because you gave up your dream job for me? I am so sorry you put your life on hold. I wish you would have told me."

"I'm practicing sharing things with you to build up my courage to talk with Joe."

A chuckle escaped Andrea.

"Do you want to work at a big accounting firm?"

"I don't know," Donna twirled her ponytail around her disappearing finger. I can't make that decision right now.

Reaching for Donna's hands, Andrea pleaded with her. "Always do what you want. I've never seen you happier than you have been with Joe, but if I misread something, don't marry him just because we think you make a great couple."

Donna abruptly stood and ran her palms down the front of her dress. "What do you say about this one?"

"You are gorgeous. If *you* like it, then get it. If not, we'll keep looking."

Ari returned as if she'd been watching the entire interaction and knew her cue. "I want this one." Her cheery voice took her by surprise.

"Let me grab the paperwork and get measurements while you pick some shoes."

Her insides had that mushy feeling she recalled as a teenager when the first boy was interested in her. Before the jaded, adult worry overpowered it, Donna pulled her phone from the front of her purse and texted Joe.

So When should we get married?

Tomorrow?

Chapter 18

DONNA USED MAKEUP TO cover the dark circles under her eyes, but her muscles felt heavy. Last night, she'd tossed and turned, wondering if Joe had been serious about marrying her. Of course, she hadn't asked. She hadn't been brave enough to share her feelings with him or ask him about his. Not yet.

Could Mom be right? Is Joe one of the good guys, or would he abandon her when she least expected it? She wiped her sweaty palms on her shirt and let out a massive breath, forcing herself to calm down. Her nerves would be the death of her.

She hadn't texted Joe back last night, nor had she seen him this morning. He couldn't be serious. Get married today? No way. Yeah, she had her dress, but they didn't have a place to get married or have a reception.

A realization struck like a Mack truck. He was still pretending. Why make this time memorable if it was all fake?

She swallowed hard, sadness cutting like a knife.

In an instant, her stomach churned. Reaching for the trash can, she emptied the contents of her stomach into the small cylinder.

What had she been thinking? They would never be a couple. Joe was her complete opposite. Every mountain, trail, and flight could be an adventure for Joe. But, for Donna, it was pure torture. She related more to ledgers, spreadsheets, and calculators.

She'd only tried everything he'd asked because she wasn't strong enough to tell people no and stick with it. She couldn't marry someone unless it was only about love.

A sigh filled the room. Donna shut her laptop just as her door whipped open. Her pulse picked up at the sight of her future husband.

Traitor. You just said you weren't marrying him. A waft of musk and cedar flooded her tiny office, melting her thought process.

"Hey, would you like to go climbing?"

Donna had loved the last time the four of them had gone climbing together. It had been the only time she hadn't been scared out of her mind. She cleared four walls. She must have been thinking too long because Joe moved into her space, pulling her attention back to him.

"Well, I planned on going for a run. Then I have to get my mom dinner."

"I could join you," Joe suggested.

"Really? What about climbing?"

Joe shrugged, "Spend time with Brent and Andrea, or be with you? Easy decision."

He hollered over his shoulder, "Brent, we're doing our own thing tonight."

"Alright, I let Andrea know," she heard Brent's muffled voice.

Catching her gaze, Joe said, "All set. Where are we running?" He crossed his arms across his chest.

His bulging muscles distracted her. She forced herself to put her laptop in her bag gently. She ordered, "Meet me at my mom's. We'll run the trail, okay?"

"I'll run wherever you want."

Wow! Joe always knew the right thing to say, but did he mean it?

She pulled her phone from her messenger bag when her text tone sounded. "I'll see you in about twenty minutes," then he was gone.

Andrea's face splashed across her screen.

You're ditching a night with me for Joe?

Geez, jealous much?

Yup. JK. I hope you have fun.

Not too much fun though.

Oh my! You're awful.

Adorn in black running tights, a form-fitting running shirt, and a sweatshirt, Donna did dynamic stretches while she waited for Joe to arrive.

Joe's big pickup pulled into her Mom's driveway. Her breath hitched when he strolled toward her. The black, breathable fabric of this shirt tugged across his well-defined chest.

If she married him, that would be her chest to cuddle with every night. *Goodness, stop thinking about Joe's chest!*

"R-Ready?" She stumbled, feeling heat rise from her neck into her face.

She blushed even more when his eyes traveled over her before addressing her question.

"Definitely."

Once they started running, Donna built up the nerve to ask, "Do you think it's weird that a doctor made a house visit last night and my mom felt great the next morning, but now she's slowly feeling like junk again?"

"I guess I hadn't thought about it, but clearly you have. What's your concern?"

Donna appreciated Joe's intent and concerned tone. "Well, I'm not sure; something just feels wrong. I mean, my mom was the poster woman for healthy women in their late fifties; she went for her annual physical, found out that her previous doctor had left the practice, and just a couple of weeks after seeing this new doctor, my mom became sick."

"When you lay it out in that timeline, yeah, something seems wrong, but..." Joe stopped running, halting Donna. "...don't kill the messenger, but are you sure you're not too emotionally close to his?" She opened her mouth to retort, but he cut her off. "I know I'd be if it were my mom."

"Of course, there's emotion, but there's also logic. That's why I wanted to get my mom to the best cancer center in the country. They are a new group of eyes to look at her, but she won't go.

"Have you told her your concern?"

She nodded, letting out a long breath. "I have. She doesn't want to hear it."

A sympathetic expression washed over Joe's face. "Do you want to head back?"

"No, thank you. I've got to let the frustration out somehow."

"I'm always here for you." Joe's smile.

Clutching her shirt's hem in her fist, she returned the smile. "I appreciate that."

About a mile further into the trail, a well-endowed woman with a size two waist running towards them flashed Joe a flirty smile. She turned around and ran in line with Joe. "I haven't seen you run this trail before."

Seriously? She was flirting with Joe right in front of Donna. Not that he was her real boyfriend, but the violent tornado picking up speed in Donna's chest seemed to think differently.

The green-eyed monster burned in Donna's chest like heartburn and acid reflux combined. She would never begrudge Joe his freedom to date since they weren't a real couple, but would he fall for this short Barbie wanna-be?

That wasn't nice, she scolded herself. She'd never been one to fight over a man, but. . .

"Are you flirting with me in front of my fiancé? How classless."

The plastic flirting queen put her hand to her chest. "I'm so sorry I didn't see you." She barely looked at Donna before she turned her attention back to Joe. "If you ever want to level up, come here again. I'm always here working on my figure." She ran her hands over her hourglass shape and then feathered her fingers down Joe's arm as she ran ahead.

What a tramp! Donna immediately looked to the sky and said, "I'm so sorry, Lord, for my thoughts."

Joe chuckled, "What were you thinking?"

"Nothing," Too ashamed to admit.

He gently tugged on her arm, bringing her to a stop. The smirk on his face let her know he wouldn't let this go.

"Are you jealous?'

"Pshaw. Don't flatter yourself. Why would I be jealous of a fake boyfriend? You're free to have any Barbie doll you want."

"You're more green than the Wicked Witch of the West."

Donna gasped, "Did you just compare me to a witch?"

"Yes, but that's not what I meant — just the color.

Donna nearly tripped on a tree root protruding from the earth in the middle of the path. Joe's quick reflexes caught Donna around the waist. He pulled her flush against his chest - she warmed instantly. She felt the erratic beating of his heart against hers, beating equally as fast. If she was being honest, her fast heartbeat had little to do with her stumble and everything to do with their proximity.

"You, good?" Joe pulled back slowly, giving her a chance to acknowledge his question and inhale his manly scent.

Realizing she was safe from falling, her death grip loosened, causing Joe's heart to frown.

"Did you just sniff me?"

A sweet pink hue flushed Donna's cheeks as Joe laced his fingers with hers.

"I think it's best if I hold your hand and we walk the rest of the way so you don't have another mishap."

"Thank you for hanging out with me tonight," Donna said as they continued down the path that was quickly losing sunlight.

Joe raked his fingers through his hair and then ran his palm over his face. She knew he was nervous about something.

"You alright?"

Pulling her to the side, Joe lifted her chin with his forefinger. "I want to marry you."

Donna's breath quickened, trying to process his sweet tone and unbelievable words.

"Let's get married on the beach on Saturday. Just your mom, Andrea, and Brent."

"What about your parents?"

"We'll invite them, but Mom won't come unless Dad does, and who knows with that man?"

"Shouldn't we discuss things?"

Joe loomed closer, and her knees turned to water. She grabbed his bicep to steady herself.

"Do you believe in Jesus?"

You know I do, Joe."

"That's all I need to know."

Heat curled down her spine at the confidence of the man she'd call her husband if she just agreed.

Like usual, fear gnawed at her insides. What if she was yet again giving in to someone else's dream or desire instead of what she really wanted? How would she know if Joe was the one?

Lord, please show me what I need to know right this second.

A last-second beam of sunlight streamed through the tree branches, illuminating Joe's smiling face. Her shoulders relaxed, and fresh energy filled her, bringing a fabulous moment of freedom to her soul.

Thank you, Lord.

"Okay. Saturday, we'll get married."

Joe punched his fist in the air.

Chapter 19

♥

JOE MARVELED AT THE thought that his parents would never discover that he and Donna had faked their relationship, and maybe his dad would respect him as a married man.

Elation filled his chest. They were on their way to his parents' house. It was about time he could give his father some exciting news. His father measured success by marrying a good woman and gaining wealth. Joe had wealth, and now he had a fabulous woman. What could go wrong?

"I haven't talked to my father since we last had dinner. I can't imagine this will go any better." Joe plopped his hand on shift while the other hand gripped the wheel so hard he feared his knuckles would pop.

Liquid fire ran through his veins when Donna placed her palm on his forearm. "Remember that you're here to invite them to your wedding — a special event — don't let the conversation veer off course."

"Easier said than done," Joe mumbled as he pulled into his parent's driveway.

"I know that's why I said it, and you have to do it."

"Gee, thanks."

She smiled and patted his arm as she released her seat-belt.

When she smiled at him like that, he could do anything, even face a room full of snakes, which he despised. He'd been bitten during one of his first hikes with Brent. Since then, Joe had kept an extra eye out for the sneaky reptile.

Her smooth fingers slid down his arm and wound their way around his. The feel of her skin made his pulse race. All he wanted to do was drive away to a secluded area and kiss her thoroughly. Her sparkly blue eyes dropped to his lips. There weren't enough harnesses in the world to protect him from falling for this woman.

Man, it was hot. He contemplated turning the car back on and letting the air conditioner blow on his face. If he kissed her right now, making out in his parent's driveway would be awkward, but he wouldn't want to stop.

"We should get this over with. Then I have something to discuss with you."

Donna gasped. "You can't drop statements like that and leave me hanging."

Having Donna by his side was like Heaven. Even if she didn't care for him the way a future wife should love her soon-to-be husband, he knew Donna felt something for him. He jogged around the car, opened her door, and wrapped his arm around her shoulders, hoping she might acknowledge the gesture with a smile or gently brush his forearm or hand. Heat seared through his shirt when she wrapped her arm around his lower back.

Marrying her wouldn't be hard at all. She was the complete package. Her stunning beauty on the outside paralleled her beauty on the inside. She was sweet, loyal, nurturing, and smart.

"I figured we should practice a few things for tomorrow."

He knew his mom would be happy to have a daughter. His mom was never the problem, but he was confident his dad would have something negative to say.

"What exact—"

"—Joe, Donna. It's great to see you both." Beverly Hartley was always a gracious host. Come in and share this news you have."

By the time they settled in the sitting room, Joe's dad had arrived. Joe listened to another one of his dad's rants about business and success but finally snapped. "What is your problem?"

He didn't care if his dad didn't think he was good enough. Brent did. That's why they had gone into business together. Even more importantly, Donna did. She always encouraged him to follow his dream and not live his life for his dad. He had to wonder if she was speaking from experience.

The elder Harley threw both his hands in the air. "Oh, I don't know. Maybe I have a problem with my only son wasting his God-given intelligence to fit harnesses on people and whatever else you do all day. You should be constructing places like Adventure Park, not working at them."

"Adventure for You," Joe corrected his dad.

His dad rolled his eyes and waved his hand dismissively.

"Oh, so Brent and I are losers for buying a business and operating it." Joe crossed his arms across his chest. "That's a new one. I wonder what John Rockefeller would say about that?"

"If you had aspirations that resembled Rockefeller's, I wouldn't mind. Go out and buy all the amusement parks you want, but be the engineer your degree says you are and construct every ride within the parks you own."

"That sounds like an awful life. Quite frankly, it sounds like your life. You work around the clock, never spend time with your family, and always think about work. I might as well drop dead now."

"Stop being dramatic," Ivan ordered. "You're mother, and I just want the best for you."

Joe snickered. "I call it realistic, not dramatic." He shook his head. "I'm sorry if you can't accept this, but that's not the life I want. Besides, I use my engineering degree as you just described, so you should be happy, yet we know nothing makes you happy unless you have money and your own way."

Joe studied his dad's face until he replied. "Son, I'm not mad at you. I'm disappointed. I know your potential, and I hate seeing you waste it."

He pinned his dad with his eyes. Any second, his knuckles and jaw might shatter from clenching them so tight.

Donna's sweet voice pulled his attention away. She had avoided eye contact with his dad but looked at his mom with reverence. "Beverly, may I use your bathroom?" Joe knew this was her need to get away before she said anything.

"Sure, Dear. Down the hall and to the left.

As soon as Donna left, Joe tried the same tactic of focusing on his mother. "I didn't come here to be ridiculed for the umpteenth time. I came to invite you to our wedding."

His mom shrieked so loud he thought she'd crack her flower vase. She bolted out of her chair and hugged him. "Oh, Joe, I'm so excited. Donna's such a nice girl."

"Harmph"

"I don't care what you think, so keep your comments to yourself." Joe had dealt with his dad's demeaning talk for years, but he wouldn't stand by and have his say one bad word about Donna.

Hands up, Ivan signaled for Joe to calm down. "What do you know about this girl? You've been dating, what, eight months?"

"I know all I need to."

He shook his disapproving head. "How does Brent feel about this? She'll get part of your business if things don't work out. Aren't you at least going to do a prenup?"

"Look, Donna is going to inherit more money than you make in a year once her mom dies, so don't ask me if I know what I'm doing."

The clearing of a woman's throat behind him hit him like a brick. He first saw his mom's sympathetic eyes. As he turned, Donna's eyes were filled with angst.

"Donna, I don't know how much you heard, but I think you misunderstood. My dad—"

"—it doesn't matter. Are we able to go now? Thank you, Mrs. Hartley."

Mrs. Hartley? What happened to Beverly?

Joe threw the invitation on the table. "I'll leave this if you want to grace us with your presence, King Hartley." He looked at his mom's dejected face. "I'll let you know if this is still on." He wanted to knock his dad's smug look off his face. Ivan had baited him, and without fail, Joe fell hook, line, and sinker.

He tried to keep up, but Donna buckled in the car before he could round the hood. This would be a long, cold ride home. He knew dealing with snakes would have been easier than visiting his dad. In a matter of twenty minutes, Ivan had ruined the little progress he'd made with Donna.

He never should have come here. That is what they make envelopes for. So what if the wedding was tomorrow? He'd claim the mail was responsible for them not getting it on time.

Lord, only you can help me out of this own. Please give me the words I need right now.

"Please don't say anything until I'm done. Women have always used me." Her eyes reached his and studied them. He hated what he saw, pity, it seemed.

"My dad was always the first to tell me I was being taken advantage of. Actually, he called me a fool more often than not." He shook the frustration that his father was correct from his head. "Anyway, he told me I needed you to sign a prenup. I assumed he was insinuating that you were using me."

Just thinking about it, Joe felt anger bubbling inside him like a volcano, ready to explode. How dare he accuse the precious woman beside him of being callous and manipulating.

"I don't want any of your money, and I know you'd never do anything to hurt Brent or me. I was trying to show *him* you will have more to lose than me. I am sorry it didn't come out right."

"Thank you for explaining. I forgive you." She gave him a genuine smile, but her eyes were marked with sadness. He didn't know what that was about, but he'd find out. From this day forth, Joe would work to take whatever pain she was hiding and whatever pain may come her way! He would be the best husband, and she'd fall madly in love with him.

"Now, what about that practice?"

Chapter 20

♥

THE RISING SUN PEAKED through the slight break in her curtain. Donna yawned and stretched. Dragging herself from bed, she tamed her wild hair, created from all her tossing and turning last night. Whenever a sickening feeling continued to pelt her in the gut — this is all pretend, she'd thought about texting Joe and calling off the wedding, but she hadn't.

He said he was doing this for her mom's benefit. Something akin to disbelief washed over her after having those thoughts. Every. Single. Time. Vulnerability and desire had shared space in his eyes every time he captured Donna's gaze. She shook off the warm, fuzzy feeling that had come over her, knowing that they were trying to fill her mom's last days with happiness.

Once her mom passed away, Joe would probably take on another death-defying adventure that she didn't have any interest in joining him on. She tried not to think about the ache in her chest whenever the notion of not being with Joe came to mind, but as she brushed her teeth, washed up, and got dressed, the pain grew deep in the cavity of her chest, thinking about all the pain she'd be enduring soon between the loss of her mom and Joe.

As Donna walked to her car, the sun's blazing light shimmered as it reflected off her windshield. Donna had told Brent and Joe that she'd work in the office a few hours this morning while her mom slept so they could help out with a big group. On her way to work, she sang at the top of her lungs to eighties rock ballads, which, in time, caused her to cry.

"Imagine a man loving a woman so much he considered her to be like *Heaven*," Donna said aloud. From Warrant to Skid Row, Donna cried even louder when the chorus of *I'll Remember You*, hit a little too close to home.

Donna wiped her eyes and turned the radio down to a reasonable volume as the Adventure for You sign appeared. Despite knowing how busy it would be today, she hadn't expected to see so many vehicles in the parking lot this early. When she entered the main building, it was empty. "Where is everyone?" She whispered. "Probably inspecting the courses," she answered herself.

A beautiful bouquet of tulips, croquis, and daffodils sat on her desk, brightening up the office space. A warm feeling filled her chest, and a smile formed on her mouth, hoping Joe had left them for her. There wasn't anyone else it could have been in her mind, but then again, she couldn't imagine Joe giving her flowers either.

Tentatively, she pulled out the card buried in the middle of her three favorite flowers. Her hands trembled as she opened the envelope and tugged on the little card. Tears pooled in her eyes as she read and reread the only sentence written.

Donna,
Marrying you will be the best adventure of my life!
Love, Joe

A light tap on her door caught her attention.

"How do you like the flowers?" His breathy voice caused her chest to rise and fall with short, rapid breaths.

No one had ever made her heart race or her skin tingle like Joe did. Was erratic breathing normal in this situation? She didn't know. In just a few steps, he was in front of her, wrapping his index finger around her pinky. That simple touch had those hawk wings flapping wildly in her stomach again, and her arm tingled with her shoulder touching the center of his chest. Despite all the action going on inside, the outside of her body stilled when he spoke.

"Thank you for agreeing to marry me. I won't let you down." His breath smelled like an orange mint. She loved oranges. The urge to taste the fruit flavor on his lips over-whelmed her like never before. What was she doing? She couldn't let her guard down now just because he sent shivers down her spine when he spoke to her, but to her surprise, she already had.

Becoming Joe's wife was looking better and better by the minute.

Chapter 21

♥

ANDREA HAD WRITTEN OUT explicit directions for Brent and Joe and they were following them perfectly. They laid tulips and croquis in a pattern, forming two lines for an aisle. This led to a small archway that Andrea had picked up yesterday. Where the men set it up, there was no fear of low tide washing it away.

Joe set up three beach chairs, one for Emily and the other two for his parents, in case they showed up.

He texted his mom last night to let her know the wedding was still on. Her response didn't surprise him—*I hope we can make it.*

Sadness rolled over him like a steamroller. He knew how much his mom wanted this moment — her only son getting married. Though it may not seem like it, this would be his only wedding. He loved Donna, and he'd show her with every adventurous muscle he had.

Instead of letting a gray, ominous, *what-if* cloud follow him around, he set the chairs and forgot them.

A chuckle escaped him as he watched Brent meticulously wrap green stuff around the archway.

"Better get used to it, you hyena. Donna will have you doing things like this before you know it. In fact, don't you have a picnic to set up?" Brent guffawed.

So far, Brent's words had been pretty accurate. His chest tightened like an uncomfortable harness, squeezing him in all the wrong places.

He could handle anything Donna asked. He'd offer to move to Texas with her; that said it all, right?

Joe spread a flowery tablecloth over the picnic table that they carried to their semi-secluded spot. Andrea had packed egg and ham salad sandwiches, fruit, chips, and chocolate chip cookies. He learned that they were Donna's favorite. As he removed the food from the wicker basket, Joe wondered if they'd ever go on a picnic, just the two of them. Would they have children who they could take on a picnic? Sometimes, Joe would want Donna to himself. A slow grin pulled at his lips. He was getting ahead of himself. She still needed to show up and marry him.

A lot depended on opening the lines of communication. If she felt half of what he did, they'd have a happily ever after until death did them part. If she didn't. . . well, he hoped it didn't come to that.

A black Lexus pulled into a spot in the small parking lot above the hill. When he saw his mom's vehicle, a burst of happiness exploded in his chest. Lingering frustration burned, too, knowing before anyone exited the sporty car that his dad wasn't with her. *His loss!*

Joe jogged up the embankment to greet his mom. "Thanks for coming."

"I wouldn't miss it for the world." She gave Joe the warmest hug.

Beverly chuckled, "I might need to find new living arrangements, but this is worth it."

Let's hope so. If this wedding ended up being a sham due to Donna's feelings, or lack thereof, he'd feel awful that his mom put so much on the line for him. Ironically, she didn't seem too affected by her statement, so maybe this would be for the best.

"Are you serious?"

"I have a bag packed in the trunk."

Joe ran his hand through his hair, messing it up even more.

"Don't do that, honey; Donna will want everything perfect for pictures."

"She likes it messy."

Beverly's shoulders bounced as she wrapped her arm around Joe's waist and rested her head on his shoulder. "Well, you're all set then."

"I'm sorry this put you in a bad spot." Joe led her toward the water.

"I'm not. If he can't accept you the way you are, I'm not accepting him."

Joe halted, turning to face his mom, "You left him. He didn't kick you out?"

"Funny thing about fear, Son, is that it's usually a hundred times worse in your head than in reality. I never stood up to him, fearing he'd kick me out or something worse, so I stayed quiet, which actually let the beast inside him grow. I am sorry I didn't stand up to him sooner. He never should have treated you that way."

Hugging his mom, Joe squeezed her tight. "You have nothing to be sorry for. I left, and he still harassed me, so your fear made sense."

After a few beats, Joe offered, "You can stay at my apartment. I'll talk to Donna about us staying at her Mom's. Joe had shared the news of Emily's terminal illness with his mom, so everyone understood Donna's desire to spend as much time as possible with her before she passed on.

"Thank you, Joe."

"Hey, Mrs H., how are you?" Brent strolled up. "How's everything look? Your son didn't do a thing. This is all my handy work."

"Liar," Joe punched Brent in the arm. "I set up the chairs and the picnic table."

"Whoa, maybe I should call the catering company down the street and tell them their prize employee got away from them." Brent punched him back.

"Alright, boys. We need completely intact tuxes for the wedding."

Frantically checking his watch, Joe stared at the slowly approaching limo. "I think my woman is arriving," he declared.

The gray clouds melted away to the brightly shining sun. *Are you telling me something, Lord?* A sunny day on your wedding day was good luck, right?

"You stay here. Andrea and Donna will kill me if you see her before it's time."

Brent rushed up the hill and opened the back door. He helped Emily out first. She held onto Brent's arm, looking weaker than she had the day before.

"Brent, shut the door before Andrea gets out," Joe yelled, running toward the stretched vehicle.

"What's wrong?" Brent questioned.

"Nothing, I just figured I could help Emily, and you'd bring Andrea. Isn't Donna staying in there until we start?

"Sounds like a plan."

Joe escorted Emily toward the water, stopping where he'd left his mom. "Emily, I'd like you to meet Beverly Hartley, my mom."

"It's a pleasure to meet you finally," Beverly stuck out her hand.

"Pish posh. I like hugs." Emily let go of Joe to embrace his mom.

"How about I get you beautiful women to your seats," Joe extended both elbows to escort the women the rest of the way.

Time ticked slowly. The pastor took his position in front of the archway. Joe swayed from side to side, wiping his brow for the fifth time. Just then, the limo door opened, revealing the most gorgeous woman in the world. He knew his life would change forever in that moment.

Joe studied Donna's every move as she worked her way down the embankment herself, an impressive feat in those shoes.

Once she reached the beginning of the flower aisle, their eyes locked. Her eyes glistened, accentuating her green eyes, which looked like a mint green sapphire in the brightly shining sun. The sun radiated on her, producing a shiny circle above her head resembling a halo — *my angel.*

For Joe, each step she took was painstakingly slow. An urge to rush down the aisle, scoop her into his arms, and carry her the rest of the way hit Joe like a tsunami.

Moments later, he extended his hand to Donna. Her small hand fit perfectly in his, sending tingles through his body. Her soft eyes put him at ease. "Thanks for showing up," Joe chuckled, half serious.

"I have another appointment at three, so we'll have to hurry this along." The corners of her mouth lifted up, letting him know she was joking.

"You look stunning."

"Welcome, everyone," the pastor started then Joe was lost in his own thoughts.

Thank you, Lord, for this breathtaking woman with whom I can share my life. Give me the strength to treat her right. Help me protect her and love her the way you expect.

"Do you have the rings?" Donna squeezed his hands, capturing his attention just in time for Joe to hear the pastor's request repeated. Everyone's boisterous laughter filled his face with heat.

"It's not my fault Donna captivates me," Joe remarked playfully, reaching into his jacket pocket for the rings.

After they shared their vows, his favorite words, which he'd been anticipating all day, poured out of the pastor's mouth.

"You may now kiss your bride."

Joe's heart thumped harder than King Kong through New York City. He pulled Donna, his wife, toward him. She fell into his chest.

"Hello," she whispered.

Unless he imagined it, he heard affection in her voice. The beating of her heart vibrated through his chest. "I've been waiting for this moment for months," he said, his fingers gripping her waist tighter.

"Joe," a blazing inferno roared in his low belly at the sound of his name purring off her lips in a sultry whisper. "what are you waiting for?"

He searched her face, looking for doubt, but it never came. A soft chuckle escaped him. "Sorry."

She grabbed his biceps and arched up as he dipped his chin. Her soft, velvety lips moved slowly with his. Not wanting to push her too fast or have a full-blown make-out session in front of their moms, Joe pulled away. Unsure of the exact comparison, he knew he sported a goofy grin and hoped no one had a camera on him.

Wedded bliss. Joe didn't care what he had to do; he'd show Donna how much he adored her!

Chapter 22

♥

"That was nice of your mom to let mine stay at her house so we could have our wedding night here." Joe sounded casual and calm while Donna's stomach gnawed on itself.

"Sure was," Donna replied dryly before shoving her toothbrush in her mouth, scrubbing with a vengeance. She'd wear the enamel clean off if she pressed the bristles any harder over the pearly whites.

She saw Joe stalk down the hall from the corner of her eye. A few moments later, he returned to the bedroom. After she rinsed off her brush, she leaned further into the sink, filled the palm of her hand with water, and swished it around.

In the time it had taken her to finish brushing her teeth, Joe had passed by the bathroom door three more times. What was he doing?

Opening the door, she stood on the threshold, waiting for him to return. As he approached, Donna stepped in his way. "I'm done with the bathroom; it's all yours."

"Thanks."

"What are you doing?"

Joe rocked on his heels with his arms crossed tightly over his chest. Donna's eyes roamed over each muscle that twitched in his arms and chest. Was he doing that on purpose? His smug look was her answer.

Donna's dry mouth became a priority. "Can I get a glass of water?"

"Sure. The glasses are in the cupboard next to the refrigerator. Would you like me to get it for you?"

"No, I'm good. Thank you."

Donna shot him a challenging look when he didn't budge. His hallway was the size of the middle aisle on a school bus, and he was a wall of muscle over six feet high and wide enough to fill the shrinking hallway.

She turned on her side to scoot by, and he pulled her wrist. "I'm glad we did this."

Donna nodded. His hot, sweet breath on her wrist as he kissed it could have given her a cavity. "Me, too," she squeaked out.

After drinking a full glass of water, she realized that Joe was making a bed on the couch. She couldn't kick him out of his bed, but she knew saying anything would be a waste of her breath, so she fought fire with fire.

Donna reminded herself of Linus from The Peanuts as she dragged every blanket Joe had behind her. She neatly folded each one for padding. At the same time, Joe tried to stop her.

"You're not sleeping out here when I have a big bed to sleep in."

"If you can, I can." For Donna, this wasn't your male, and I'm female. Anything you can do, I can do too. Nope. This was different. Joe had slowly returned to his fun-loving joking ways, and she liked it and wanted to be close to him.

A few moments after settling in, Donna smiled and let out a little sigh, knowing she won this battle.

She heard movement and turned to investigate. Joe sat up, ramrod straight.

"What are you doing? Donna gasped as Joe reached behind him, pulled his t-shirt over his head, and tossed it on the floor.

"I sleep in boxer shorts." The smirk pulling at his lips told Donna that he was enjoying torturing her.

"Nice try, but you won't get rid of me that easy." Donna laid back down, feeling proud of her boldness.

"No? Well, since you found it necessary to follow me to the living room, feel free to continue."

"I'm not sleeping without my shirt on."

Joe shrugged, "It was worth a shot, wifey." His sweet voice vibrated through Donna's chest.

"Good night, Joe."

"Why are women so stubborn?"

"How many stubborn women have you had?" Donna's face burned at the question, not really wanting to know.

"You'd be the first."

"Then how do you know that women — plural — are stubborn?"

"Men talk."

"Oh, so you *men* have classified women as stubborn. Interesting."

"Dare I ask what's "interesting"?

"If memory serves me correctly—"

"—I'm sure it does; women remember everything too."

She let out an exaggerated breath.

"As I was saying, you're out here for the same reason I am. Neither of us wanted the other to be inconvenienced. Both, trying to make the other feel comfortable, so that makes you stubborn, too."

"I was being a gentleman. You may be my wife, but I know you don't want to sleep with me, and I'm not making you sleep on this ratty old couch."

She swallowed hard as if getting ready to speak. His thoughtfulness sent a ripple of warm sensations through her body.

"No comeback?"

She sighed in a singsong, sarcastic tone, "Aw, that's so sweet. You are such a gentleman."

He threw a pillow at her, but she caught it; his eyes widened, "Nice."

"For the record, either were both stubborn, or we're both kind and considerate." She took his pillow and stuffed it under her head.

"Fine. Can I have my pillow back now?"

"Nope."

"Are you serious? I don't have one. So much for being considerate."

"And a gentleman would never point out that me using a pillow you gave me in your oh-so-gentlemanly way would need to be returned. Her chuckle and smug tone sounded like *gotcha, one point for Donna.*

Joe's thunderous laughter, music to Donna's ears, filled the room.

"Well, darling, if you don't give me my pillow back in the next three seconds, I'm going to come get it in the most gentlemanly way I know how. One."

Donna's heart beat out of control. Her chest constricted. Something akin to a panic attack brewed in her chest. Part of her nervousness was the unknown. What would he do? She trusted Joe completely, so she wasn't scared of him in someone's going to kill her sort of way. But the idea that this man was now her husband and her attraction to him filled her entire being, that was terrifying. *Breathe!*

"Two. I'm not joking. I'll get that pillow one way or another."

Why didn't she just give it to him? Donna liked the shutter her body produced when she slipped by Joe in the hallway earlier. The feel of his strong fingers tenderly holding her wrist — *Oh man!*

"Three."

Before Donna could register what was happening, Joe was straddling her hips, ticking her sides. She squirmed side to side, laughing. "Stop, please," she begged in between ragged breaths.

His hands froze in mid-air. "Are you going to give me my pillow?" Their eyes locked. His were intense yet playful.

"No."

Without warning, he was at it again. "Stop, for real. You're going to make me pee my pants."

"You'll be sleeping without pants then." His tone showed no mercy, but she knew he'd feel bad if it happened.

"Stop being so stubborn, woman, and give me my pillow."

He grabbed a hold of her wrists and pinned her to the floor. He leaned forward, and the pressure from his muscular chest brought her comfort as her chest heaved, trying to recover from the loss of oxygen.

"You have the most mesmerizing eyes I've ever seen."

"He continued to lean closer. The beating of his race heart captured her attention. The smoldering look in his eyes made her feel desired, wanted, something she'd never felt before. They hadn't talked about the sleeping arrangements during this marriage. But

"I'll be taking that." He casually pulled the pillow — his pillow — from under her head. "Thank you, beautiful." Before she knew what happened, he kissed her forehead and hopped back onto the couch."

"You big jerk." Donna wanted that kiss.

"I told you I'd get my pillow."

"Ah, so pretending you were interested was your method. I forgot what a great actor you are."

"That wasn't an act. You're my wife. I'm interested in all sorts of things, and once you are, there'll be no stopping me. I think I proved that point just a few minutes ago."

Donna couldn't speak. *What the heck just happened? So apparently, Joe, my husband, really wanted to marry me.*

Her blood started to boil, thinking about his admission. They'd start acting like husband and wife as soon as she was ready. He really was a gentleman, and he was hers.

Chapter 23

♥

JOE ACCEPTED THE DAY'S invitation. A day of new beginnings, the first step, per sé, in the journey he planned to trek with Donna.

The soft orange and pink hues of the sky surrounded the radiant golden rays of the sun peeking beyond the horizon. "Thank you, Lord, for this mesmerizing reminder of your presence." Joe started praying aloud as he drove. It wasn't like he could close his eyes and let the force lead him. God and everyone driving on the road definitely wanted Joe to keep his eyes open.

It seemed weird that he'd be heading into work the day after his wedding, but they decided a honeymoon later on would be better for the business and spending time with Emily. After last night, Joe hoped he'd have a traditional honeymoon all in good time.

He'd seen the desire in her eyes and was proud of himself for being vulnerable. Barring his heart wasn't easy for him. If he didn't know better, that was when he noticed Donna's shift. His dad had always told him, "Never show weakness; you'll get eaten alive."

Perhaps that's the case in the business world, but with a woman like Donna, she seemed to appreciate it. Thinking of her brushing up against his body, her body underneath his, her wrists under his hands — *whoa!* Joe rolled his window down, letting the cool, morning air rush in.

Leaving Donna this morning had taken all his strength. He felt like she was orbiting in his world, but she was just out of his reach. He tried to focus on getting coffee while she made them scrambled eggs and toast. Everything had felt different since he'd revealed his true feelings. When the coffee had started cascading down the side of the cup, scorching his hand, he'd winced, setting the mug down quickly.

A blister had formed instantly despite running it under warm water. Perhaps his hand had yet to cool down since Donna's slender fingers had held it under the stream of water from the tap. Looking at the gauze she'd taped to his hand, he smiled as he recalled her touch.

The shiny, black Mercedes parked in the visitor's lot at work let Joe know their potential investors had arrived early. Today, Joe needed to wow these execs into investing half a million dollars to help make his dream of creating the world's steepest zip-line come true.

His phone buzzed, notifying him of a text. Hoping it was Donna, he rushed to grab it from the cupholder. Disappointment painted his face at the sight of his dad's name instead. He groaned, wondering if he should even look. Against his better judgment, he did. The phrase *sucker for punishment* came to mind.

I hope you are happy. Your mother refuses to take my calls.

For the first time in his life, Joe didn't feel the need to respond or fight for his dad's acceptance. There was no denying his love for Donna; the look of desire he'd seen in her eyes last night had given him this confidence.

Yet, he wanted to stand up for himself once and for all.

I'm not taking your abuse anymore, either. This is my send-off before blocking you. Have a nice life.

Before he could change his mind, Joe blocked his father's number. His mouth curved into a gigantic smile. After years of taking his belittling and criticizing, Joe didn't worry about how long this would be; he relished the freedom he'd gained by removing his dad's toxic words from his life. Hopefully, his mom would feel liberated, too.

"Mr. Hartley, Mr Smith, we are excited to back this project. My secretary will send over the final paperwork next week. If that's okay with you, I will include language that my grandson gets to be the first to try it out." Mr. Walton winked at Joe while simultaneously gripping his hand firmly.

"He can be one of the first, but I don't let anyone try out my zip lines until after I've taken the first ride."

"Joe's number one priority is safety," Brent added as he shook the investor's hand.

Mr. Walton smiled. "I love hearing that. We just pulled out of a six-billion-dollar project with S&J when one of the coasters they designed failed safety protocols, yet they cleared it anyway."

Brent and Joe shared a look, then plastered fake smiles on their face while walking the man to his car.

"Thanks again. I see great things coming your way, gentlemen," Mr. Walton said, lifting his chin to acknowledge Joe and Brent, then ducked into his car.

Once the man's car left the lot, Brent shifted his attention to Joe. Are you okay with what we just learned?"

"Is he so ruthless that he doesn't care about people's lives? Who does a thing like that?"

"You're dad, apparently."

"I don't have time to deal with his problems. I've got to call my mom on my way home and check on Donna. She's been obsessed." Joe pulled out his phone when it buzzed in his pocket. "Text number twenty-three today. She thinks the doctor is trying to kill her mom."

"Honey, I'm home," Joe called as he opened the front door to his mother-in-law's house.

His fun-loving greeting was cut short when he heard raised voices coming from Emily's room.

Joe pushed open the door. A quick search of the room revealed the problem, but he wouldn't assume anything when his wife looked so distraught.

"What is going on in here?" All three started talking at once, so Joe put his hand up to stop them.

"Donna, tell me what's happening."

"Gladly. Dr. Campbell is trying to give my mom some shot of who-knows-what in the name of healthcare, but something is wrong."

Joe looked at Emily with questioning eyes.

"I called him, Joe." Looking at her daughter, she continued, "First, you want to bring me halfway across the country for treatment; now you're preventing me from getting treatment."

"It's not treatment; you said so yourself."

The doctor, whom Joe has not been introduced to, spoke up. "Your mother asked for something to take the pain away."

"Perhaps we should get hospice here," Donna challenged the man. "Yes, I'll look into that so you won't be needed any longer.

"Donna, this is still my home until I die. The doctor stays."

With tears in her eyes, Donna pushed past Joe as she exited the room.

"I understand and respect your decisions, but Donna seems sincerely concerned that you're making mistakes. Would you like me to see the doctor out before I check on Donna?"

Time seemed to stand still. Emily stared at him as if contemplating her options. If she took any longer, he would leave, determined to find Donna.

"I'm all set. Thank you, Joe."

He didn't know her well but thought her eyes were saying something different. Nonetheless, his priority was making sure his wife was okay.

Joe found Donna in the kitchen, pressed against the counter, crying over the sink. He slid his arms around her waist, pulling her flush against his chest. "How can I help?"

She shrugged her shoulders, hiding her hung head in her hands. "I know he's doing something to her, and she won't listen."

Frustration burned inside of him. Not towards Donna, but her mom and the doctor; everyone causing his wife pain right now was on his trash list.

He stepped around her and gently tugged her wrists away from her face. Joe lightly wiped a few plump teas with his thumb, then pulled her close, letting his shirt absorb the rest.

The question running through his mind was bound to get her angry, but it had to be asked if he expected to understand her concerns and help her.

"How do you know?" he didn't finish his question, knowing she understood, when her head whipped off his chest, leaving him with a chill.

Her glaring eyes unraveled Joe slightly. He'd never seen Donna as an intimidator, but right now, she reminded him of an angry football player ready to take his head off.

Her trembling hands retrieved her phone from her pocket. She pulled up different articles suggesting Dr. Campbell exploited his patient's trust to fill his pockets. One article estimated the doctor received over one million dollars in kickbacks from pushing AmbioLexon, a drug that's been found to fill perfectly healthy individuals with cancer before they knew what hit them.

"Have you shown your mom this?"

Not the right question. He put his hands up. "Of course you did, and it didn't go well."

Donna shook her head. Yanking on the sides of her shirt, she pulled Joe against her, resting her cheek on his chest.

"Are you okay? Your heart is a helter-skelter beating mess."

"Let's see; I've got the most beautiful woman in the world in my arms, *my wife*," he emphasized with a grin. "crying in my arms and this new information that someone might be trying to kill my new mother-in-law, I've got a lot of emotions running through me right now."

"Yeah, which ones specifically?" She looked up at him. Her eyes, more green than blue today, held a little mischief in them.

"Adrenaline is urging me to hunt down that doctor and rearrange his face while other feelings are wrapped up in you."

Instead of shying away like usual, Donna pushed to her toes, gaining at least four inches, so now their mouths were in line. Could this be their moment? Her breath blended with his. The kiss they'd shared at their wedding had been just enough to kickstart his heart. Now, he wanted more.

"Donna," a desperate plea left his lips, making sure this was really what she wanted. She leaned closer; their lips grazed each other just as the front door shut, pulling their attention away from what Joe had hoped would be just the warm-up.

"Sorry," her feet flat against the floor again before she gave him a disappointed look.

"Let's go check on your mom; perhaps we'll have to call the police."

Chapter 24

Despite the freedom of working from home, Donna woke at dawn to complete her work so she could spend most of the day with her mom. She'd received an email from an attorney who worked on malpractice cases. Interestingly, she'd discovered that the first lawyer she had spoken with had been connected to Dr. Campbell. What were the odds?

Now that Dr. Campbell was on the run, Donna knew whatever he had done to her mother had been shady. Hopefully, everything could be figured out before irreversible damage was inflicted on her mom

Given Emily's mild pain today, they'd visited Joe at work in the afternoon. The dark circles around her mom's eyes had told Donna it might not have been a great idea, but Emily's relentless pestering had worn Donna down, telling her it was good practice for becoming a mom.

That thought almost paralyzed her. She and Joe had been married for less than a week. Donna wasn't ready to talk about having children. Heck, she still hadn't opened up to Joe like he'd done with her. Could she stop worrying that he'd leave her? He said he'd be patient and wait for her.

Those words, like springtime flowers, bloomed in her chest.

She'd already been crazy attracted to him, but the more she got to know him, the less her attraction was linked to his incredibly handsome features. The way he held her made her feel protected and cared for, like what she said and thought mattered.

When Donna and her mom entered the lobby, Joe's face was filled with an immense smile. Watching him fit guests with harnesses intrigued her. She admired the way he could explain the safety rules and secure their safety simultaneously, demonstrating his undeniable skill and knowledge, making *her husband* even more appealing.

While Donna asked guests for their opinions about the park and had them sign a release so she could post them on the website, Joe was working with a young girl; Donna guessed she was about five. She listened to the tenderness in his voice and watched the gentle way he lifted her to clip onto the line. 'Give it a good pull with those Hulk muscles,' he joked, making the little girl giggle. Twelve stories above the ground, she looked more comfortable than Donna ever had.

His voice reached her. "Are you ready?" The little girl shook her head. "Get ready to fly!" They counted down from three, and Joe let the little lady soar. She whooped and hollered like this was the best thing she'd ever done.

An image of Joe and his future daughter flooded her brain, making her cheeks flush when their eyes met. The thought comforted her, knowing that Joe would teach their daughter to be fearless and strong.

Their daughter? When did that happen? Good grief, she needed to focus on figuring out how to help her mom before she worried about having babies.

The sun's blazing light shimmered in her reflective, teary eyes as Joe turned to her mom and lifted her onto the cable like he had the little girl. Emily laughed it off and playfully slapped his shoulder. Once she hooked herself on and did the safety check, she spotted Donna.

What was going on!?

Brent appeared next to her. "She wanted to go, don't get mad at me."

"I'm not mad, just surprised."

Like the little girl before her, Emily filled the air with her enjoyment as she zoomed along the line until her voice was faint in the distance.

Happiness streaked through Donna like a comet as she watched her mom enjoy this moment. Had someone's greed shortened her mom's time with her?

Oh, Goodness, don't cry. The last thing she needed was for Joe to see her distress — too late. His brow knitted, and the concern in his eyes warmed her all over. She gave him her best smile, pulled open the back door, and entered the empty storefront.

Her office door was only ten steps away. She almost made it before Brent stopped her. "He's good with the kids, isn't he?"

Shoot. Donna hung her head, trying to avoid looking at Brent, who'd followed her. "Older women, too," she laughed.

"He'll treat you like a princess."

Brent was telling her anything she didn't already know. She raised her head and met his eyes.

"Are you okay?" Brent asked concerned.

That was all it took for her tears to freefall. "He is incredible," Donna choked out.

Donna wondered if Joe had already shared their fake dating scheme. Something in Brent's eyes confirmed what she was thinking, but she wouldn't offer any information just in case she was misreading him.

"I'm sorry. This thing with my mom . . ." her voice trailed off.

When she tried to escape, Brent gently reached out and stopped her. "Andrea, myself, and especially Joe — we're all here for you." His hand dropped to his side.

"Thank you," she whispered as she retreated to her office.

A short while later, the door flung open. "That was awesome!" Her mom's tired look overshadowed the excitement in her voice.

"Mom, you look. . . . exhausted." Donna darted out of her chair and assisted her mom to the closest seat. Joe appeared in the doorway. "How could you let her get so worn out."

Joe looked behind himself and then back at Donna. He pressed his finger into his chest. "Me?" Joe's shocked expression almost made Donna's smile. The word cute would diminish his handsomely rugged good looks, but his pleasant countenance distracted her from how awful her mom looked.

That can't happen. *Focus, Mom, is what matters!*

He cleared his throat and smugly stated, "I'm glad you think I'm powerful enough to dictate what your mother does, but you'd be sadly mistaken. No one around could tell Miss Emily what to do, nor would I try."

"Smart man," Emily laughed just before she went into a coughing fit.

Joe joined Donna beside her mother. "What do you need?" Joe's voice filled with concern.

With him so close, Donna could smell his alluring woodsy scent. That, combined with his arm and thigh brushing up against her as he swayed or moved positions, messed with her focus.

"Space." Emily shooed them away with her hands.

Her coughing episodes had become more frequent in the last few days. Reality was starting to seep in, and Donna's mom's imminent death was squeezing tight around her like the harness she'd worn skydiving. Right now, Donna expected to lose her breakfast, just like she had then.

"I'm going to show the guys the progress I've made on the website and then I'm taking you home." Donna kissed her mom on the top of the head.

It only took a few minutes to share the site. "If you want to change anything, please text me, but I need to get my mom home now."

"Nothing needs to be changed. My wife, the amazing web-site designer extraordinaire, nailed it." The affirmation warmed her heart, and her cheeks flushed.

"He's right. I'm so glad we are not losing you to some place in Texas. Excuse me," Brent said as he helped Emily into the car.

Guilt rushed through Donna. She forced a smile, hoping they didn't see it on her face, and she shut her lid. "I should get my mom home."

"Please wait." his breathy voice caused her chest to rise and fall with short, rapid breaths.

No one had ever made her feel like Joe did. Was erratic breathing normal in this situation? She didn't think so. He wrapped his index finger around her pinky. Those hawk wings flapped wildly in her gut again, and her arm tingled with her shoulder touching the center of his chest. Despite all the action going on inside, the outside of her body stilled.

"Are you okay?"

"Yeah, fine, why?"

"You just got a weird look on your face when we mentioned Texas." He dipped his head to capture her eyes. I won't let you down. I meant every word I said about being patient." His breath smelled like an orange mint. She loved oranges. The urge to taste the fruit flavor on his lips overwhelmed her like never before.

Donna would never complain about marrying Joe. He was smart, funny, and hot — there wasn't a better word to describe his rugged good looks. This was the best decision she'd ever made in her personal life. If she planned on staying married to him, she needed to let Ms. Littleton know that she wouldn't be taking the job in Texas. She'd never make Joe move. His life was here. The fact that he would move to be with her said it all.

"I'm leaving in about twenty minutes. I'll grab some Chinese food and bring it home for dinner." Joe's finger brushed the inside of her forearm, sending more electricity into her already electrified body. "Would you like something different?"

Donna dared look at him. His large, black pupils flared. *Thank you, Lord, for this man.* She'd never been more attracted to another man in her life. Rick was cute in a preppy kind of way, but Joe. His manly features and sweet gestures invaded her thoughts around the clock.

"No. Thank you, though."

"Okay. I'll see you in a little while." Joe leaned in and kissed her temple.

Oh my goodness! Breathe. His strong, robust lips lingered but not long enough. When he pulled back, the side of her head cooled instantly.

She'd get answers from him, tonight. *Why did he marry me, knowing I haven't wholeheartedly embraced his crazy adventures?* Most importantly, she would have to share her feelings with him and find out his intentions with their marriage. *Lord, give me the strength to be vulnerable.*

Chapter 25

♥

WHEN JOE ARRIVED AT Donna's mom's house, he nearly dropped the bag of Chinese food when she opened the door. Her hair hung in a loose ponytail low on her neck. Wisps of blonde locks pulled free at the sides. She wore a baggy pair of sweatpants and a sweatshirt that drowned her. The same fruity scent that had drawn him in before now invaded his senses as he walked past her, setting the food on the coffee table. He stuffed his hands in his pockets once he released the bag to prevent himself from pulling Donna into his chest and kissing her for the rest of the night. The temptation and desire overwhelmed him.

This was his life. She was his wife. How long would this last? *Forever*, he hoped.

He hadn't noticed her wearing any makeup earlier, but now her lips were shiny, and her eyelashes were darker. Did she put makeup on to impress him? *Now, that's what I'm talking about.* Not that Donna needed makeup, but the thought of her doing something to get his attention made him believe she had feelings for him.

She loved this woman more than he'd loved anyone. He didn't want anything from Emily except her daughter. Donna's mom had offered Joe everything to get married before she passed. He didn't want money, her car, her life insurance. He just wanted the beauty standing in front of him.

A knot in Joe's stomach had rooted and spread over the last week. He was worried that Donna might doubt the sincerity of his proposal.

"I'll go get my mom. She wanted to watch television in her room." Donna dashed from the room.

A few moments later, Emily appeared with Donna. "Smells delicious. Did my new Son-in-Law listen when I said how much I wanted Chinese?" Emily's entire face smiled.

"I sure did."

Donna grabbed plates, spoons for scooping, and forks and set them on the coffee table. After plating his food, he sat next to Donna on the sofa. Their closeness rocked his insides. He leaned even closer. "I'm glad you ate a little something." he gestured to the stick that once held beef teriyaki.

"She rarely eats dinner," Emily interjected.

Donna sighed. She and her mother had often had this conversation. "I eat when I'm hungry. I usually eat a late lunch."

Joe bit back a laugh. That wasn't a good enough explanation for not eating dinner. He could eat lunch, a late lunch, and dinner. He loved food, but not as much as being with his wife.

It only took Donna and Joe twenty minutes to clean up the leftovers. Donna fretted over her mother and her lack of appetite, and an air of despair filled the room. Joe knew that he'd have to console Donna when her mom finally left this life.

"I'm going to get something that Andrea sent over. I'll be right back," Joe announced.

"Thank you for dinner, Joe, but I'm going to head to my room," Emily responded, "see you kids in the morning."

When Donna appeared in the doorway, his eyes roamed over her. She dipped her head, and her cheeks grew pink. Watching her inch her way over to the sofa was pure agony. This woman had his heart; he just needed to know how she felt about him. He'd finally married the woman for him, but he needed to wait patiently for her.

"What's in the bag," she asked, her eyes wide and voice hesitant as she lowered herself to the sofa.

She had every reason to be nervous. Andrea had sent this home. He smiled, recalling the last time Andrea had them playing a game — Donna had ended up with her hand on his abs for almost an hour. *Heaven.* That was the only word that came to his mind.

"Want to play a game?" he reached for the bag.

"Oh, great. It's probably one of her fifty-question games. You know she stipulates crazy kissing and trust exercises to accompany the questions, right?"

"Well, alrighty then. Let's get to it." He rubbed his hands together and pumped his eyes at Donna, enjoying the sweet smile and tinge of pink that had started forming on her cheeks.

He pulled the games out one at a time, reading the titles. "Get to Know Your Kissing Partner." He set that box next to him. "I vote for this one."

"You haven't even seen the others yet," Donna chuckled.

"I can't imagine a game any better," Joe held her gaze for a brief moment before returning his attention to the bag of games.

"Truth or Dare for Friends." He dismissed this game. One, they'd already played a version of it, and two, he wanted Donna to see them as more than friends. He wanted their marriage to mean the same to her as it did him.

When he pulled out the last game, his mouth curved into a playful smile. "Yeah, We're Newlyweds." He held it up for Donna to see. "I'm willing to try it if you are."

"Sure," she half shrugged.

He extended the cards toward her. "Would you like to read first?"

Their bare skin connected, sending a surge of joy through his veins. He felt like a teenager, not a grown man married to the woman on the sofa. *Oh, man, w*hat he would give to hold her close.

Donna tucked a loose strand of hair behind her ear. "Answer carefully," She warned. "Do you want kids, and if so, how many?"

"Talk about killing me from the beginning," Joe cringed slightly.

"Yeah, I want kids, at least one boy and one girl; the rest are negotiable," He smirked.

"You mean you'd keep trying until you have at least one of each?" he noticed a hint of concern in her voice.

Joe shrugged. "I guess. Maybe. I honestly haven't thought too much about it."

If he wasn't mistaken, Donna let out a breath of what he thought was relief.

Donna put the card face up on the table and moved closer to him. His heart thumped against his rib cage as she inched ever so slowly in his direction. She picked up his hand. His fingers felt like a hot poker had stabbed them.

Was she breathing as fast as he was? Donna leaned in as she lifted his hand to her lips.

"What are you doing?" He choked on his words. *Nice work, Joe. How embarrassing.*

Showing him the card in her hand, Donna held it up for him to read. "The number of children your partner wants is the number of seconds you must kiss them. You choose where."

Donna's lips met the back of his hand. Her moist lips felt like a dream. He wished she'd chosen his lips or neck, but the electric current running through his hand revealed how much he liked her touching him.

When she released, Joe grabbed her hand. "That was only one second."

Donna playfully swatted him. "Nice try."

He noticed that Donna had not moved back to her side of the sofa. Joe liked this game already.

"My turn." He grabbed a card, read it, and tried to put it back.

"Oh no, that's not allowed. Whatever card you pick, you keep."

"Who says?"

"Andrea. She made the game, remember?"

"Fine. Just know I tried to put this back," Joe huffed out a breath before he read. "What non-sexual things do I do to turn you on?"

"Does it really say that?"

As she leaned closer, he felt the heat radiating from her body as she slowly read the card.

Time ticked by. It felt like hours to Joe's fragile ego, but it was probably only about one minute. "Please tell me there are too many things, and you're trying to narrow it down."

Donna giggled and turned away. "When you helped that little girl and my mom get situated on the zipline."

"That's it?"

A boisterous laugh escaped her. "Do we really have to do this?"

"No, but I am fully invested."

Donna sighed. "You have a low, deep, almost raspy tone when you've whispered things to me, so I don't know if it the voice, or the things you've said, or both, but. . ." She didn't finish her sentence before moving to another thought. "I like it when you hold me with all those muscles you have." Donna's rose-red face made him feel wanted. He felt bad. She was utterly embarrassed to tell her hubby that he was strong and she wanted him near her.

"Booyah! She likes my muscles."

"That's the one that gets you excited?" Donna shook her head playfully as he flexed his biceps. "Do you have to do anything else?"

"During the next round, rub your partner's feet." He pressed his back against the soft backing and patted his thigh. "Put 'em up here."

"You don't have to do this." She pulled her bottom lip in as she raised her eyes to meet his gaze.

He hated seeing her so nervous. If he didn't know better, he'd think she'd finally fallen for her husband, which he assumed caused her skittish behavior.

"Sure, I do. It's the game." He wagged his eyebrows, forcing her to laugh. Then his voice deepened, the one she said turned her on, and he gently pulled her shoulder toward him, causing her head to turn toward him. "Besides, I want to."

She drew in a long breath. Squeezing her eyes shut and grabbing the next card, she placed her feet on his legs and read the next question.

"What is a relationship dealbreaker for you?"

Joe smiled when a little moan escaped from Donna. "I'm glad you're enjoying this."

She pulled her feet back. "We don't have to follow the rules exactly."

He grabbed her calves and stopped her legs in midair. "I was being sincere. I like that I'm doing something you enjoy."

"Thank you. It is really nice." Donna relaxed her legs.

Nerves hit Joe. "A dealbreaker for me. . . someone who's using me or trying to control or manipulate me. I've had enough of that with the females from my past and my father."

Donna's eyes softened as she leaned forward. "How is that whole situation going?"

"Mom's still camped out in the apartment. She's been talking to him but said he's not listening. He's too busy dealing with attorneys."

Joe had told Donna about his legal trouble. Why would his dad put people's lives in danger? He couldn't even fathom the idea.

"Alright, last question, and it's bedtime." Donna swiped the card from the table.

"That's mine, thank you," he said, swiping it from her fingers.

Her playful huff matched her sweet smile — the one he'd love to kiss right now. *Focus!*

"I have to share my three secret fantasies with you." He smiled as he continued rubbing Donna's feet.

"They're not different from most committed men. I fantasize about having a wife who truly loves me and children I enjoy raising." He stilled for a long moment. "My last fantasy. . . " The anguish seeped from his eyes while she looked on, truly interested.

". . . is that I'll figure out what's wrong with me, so my dad stops. . ."

Joe's stomach lurched like he was free falling. He didn't finish his sentence, worried he sounded like a wuss.

Donna didn't give him a chance. She tossed the card to the table, dropped her legs, and slid close, angling him toward her. "There isn't anything wrong with you." Joe scoffed, hanging his head. "Hey, look at me." He lifted his chin until their eyes locked. His stomach wobbled, seeing the sincerity in her ocean blues. "You are amazing. I'm happy to call you my husband."

His voice was low and soft. "I'm yours for as long as you'll have me."

"Same."

With that one word, he longed to kiss her. She ran her tongue over her soft and alluring bottom lip and pulled it in with her teeth. This brain felt like mush. He ran his hands up her thighs and rested on her waist. Lowering his forehead onto hers, he whispered, "Donna. Thank you for taking a chance on me.

Her hand slid up his chest and gripped his shoulder, leaving a tingling burn in its wake. But then she did the unexpected. Donna, his wife, pulled him closer and brushed her lips against his for only one point three seconds before she pulled away, leaving him grinning like an idiot.

He didn't get to explain how their marriage came about, but that would come soon. Right now, Donna had blown his mind.

Chapter 26

DONNA RUBBED HER ARMS, trying to warm herself — not that she was actually cold. It was a coping mechanism whenever she was stressed or overly frustrated. She was on the verge of tears, with a pit in the bottom of her stomach gnawing viciously.

Emily's appetite had significantly waned over the past two days, a clear sign that whatever had been injected into her was taking its toll.

Then, early this morning, Donna had received a call from the detective they'd spoken to a few days before. The news was not good. Dr. Campbell had been spotted in Mexico, evading the police once again.

Good news. The authorities were still following his trail, so they said it would only be a matter of time.

She'd tried to come to terms with her mom dying, but no matter how hard she had tried to prepare herself, she knew it wouldn't matter when the end came. On top of that, she had to deal with the fact that the man who'd tried to kill her mom was still on the loose.

"Are you okay?" Joe asked, sitting up from the floor. Donna had given up the argument about who'd sleep on the floor this time. She let Joe win this one.

"Just peachy," Donna said, burying her head in her hands, deflating slightly. It was a Bald-faced lie, and they both knew it.

The mattress sunk, drawing her attention to the movement. There Joe sat, shirtless, with his hand out for her to hold.

Glancing at it quickly, Donna hesitantly slid her miniature hand into his massive, calloused hand, making him seem like a man's man.

Her eyes stalked his perfectly muscular abs and chest before landing on his kissable lips. She'd known since last night when she'd finally allowed herself to kiss her husband for mere pleasure that she wanted to kiss him every night from that day forward.

As she looked at him now, Donna wondered if she was enough for him and pulled away.

"It's okay to be vulnerable with me. I'm your husband," Joe said with a knowing smile, dipping his head to capture her eyes.

Donna stared at her phone. Her stomach flipped. "That monster got away. Detective Hernandez lost him in Mexico, but supposedly, they are still tracking him." She had her doubts.

He curled a finger under her chin. She cringed at the pity she saw in his eyes, granting her pooled tears permission to fall.

Joe hoisted Donna onto his lap in one fell swoop, ignoring her quiet yelp. How could his man smell like cedar first thing in the morning?

Resting her head against his chest, she feigned a breathing technique to calm herself down when, in fact, she was smothering her senses with all things Joe.

Besides his scent, the feel of his rippling muscles made her feel protected. The sweet words he breathed in her ear also helped her feel protected and loved. Could it be possible Joe loved her? She didn't have time for that conversation right now, but soon they would.

"Things will work out. You know God's got this. All things work together for good to those who love God, to those who are the called according to *His* purpose."

Lifting her head, her eyes roamed over his expression. She first spied the smirk, pulling at his lips. *What was there to smirk about?*

But all too quickly, concern washed over him. Were her thoughts and feelings that transparent? When her eyes traveled down to where this handsome man held her wrist, she wanted to self-destruct like Ethan Hunt's mission announcements once he accepted them.

Then, light a bolt of lightning, an idea flashed in her mind. "I know what to do."

"That's not going to happen." Joe ran his palm over his face, pacing behind the sofa as Detective Hernadez and his partner, Detective Garcia, expanded upon Donna's plan.

Sitting in the adjacent chair, Donna drank Joe in. His bicep and tricep bulged as he extended his arm and then curled his arm to run his hand through his hair. With each step, even his leg muscles popped out from underneath his athletic shorts. She definitely married up.

She hated the turmoil etched on his face. With every twitch of his jaw, she saw his concern. In a roundabout way, this moment solidified things for Donna. She felt loved, finally loved, and she couldn't wait to tell Joe — no, she couldn't wait to *show* Joe how much she loved him too.

Her feelings had grown. Honestly, how could they not? They'd spent time faking their relationship to help their friends, but she'd fallen for him before they'd even left for Hawaii, which is why his dismissal hurt so much.

But when she thought back, in words, he'd said they shouldn't be together, but not in action, and everyone knows that actions speak louder than words. He'd pursued her despite her making it difficult.

"Mr. Hartley, I can understand your concern. I'd feel the same way if it were my wife. But look at this from her perspective. The man tried to kill her mother. The new evidence reveals that he's working with or for someone else. She has the opportunity to save many lives."

"Do you mind if I speak with my wife in the kitchen?"

"Not at all. Go right ahead," both detectives spoke at once.

Pressing his hand to the small of her back as he led her into the kitchen caused her breath to hitch.

She hadn't planned any of this — falling in love with Joe, marrying him, planning an undercover mission to catch villains out to kill perfectly healthy people for money.

"Please tell me, you've rethought this crazy idea and won't put yourself at risk."

Donna crossed her arms, glaring at the man in front of her. "This is a good plan to catch the people trying to kill my mother. You would do this if it were your mother, right? I'd hope so."

'Yes, I would, but that's me, my life. I don't want to risk your life."

"Oh, so it's okay if you die and leave me here to mourn you, but it's not okay being flipped around."

She saw Joe contemplating her words, probably choosing his next words very carefully."

"At the risk of sounding insensitive based on how you put it, yes. I'm supposed to keep you safe. How am I supposed to do that in this situation?"

"Pray. Truly, only God can keep me safe. What was that you said earlier? All things work together for good to those—"

"— yeah, yeah, Joe interrupted. Is this how marriage will go — you using my good points against me?"

"At the risk of sounding insensitive. . ." he shook his head and crossed his arms over his chest as Donna yet again used his words for her own purpose: ". . .yes, only when applicable, though."

The corners of Donna's lips tugged upward in a suggestive smile. She slid her arm over Joe's strong arms, up his chest, and around his shoulders before wrapping her hand at the back of his neck where her fingers ran through his hair, massaging his scalp, forcing a light moan to escape Joe's mouth.

"Joe," her voice had never sounded so passionate.

His dark eyes dipped, focusing on her lips. She moistened them with her tongue in the event he would actually kiss her this time. When their eyes fastened again, she lost her train of thought.

Joe's fingers hooked onto her hip, and he took a slight step forward. All breathy, he whispered, "I won't want to stop once you give me the green light, so be certain of your next words.

She leaned even closer, feeling his stubble drag across her cheek. Inches from his ear, she whispered, "Joe, I'm going undercover."

Pushing her hips back, his scowl was undeniable, like disappointment slapped across the face. His shoulders slumped.

"I'm scared." Donna let out a full breath, deflating her lungs. If she hadn't already fallen in love with Joe, she would have with those two words. Any man willing to share honest emotions was a keeper.

"I get it. Me too." He pulled her in for a hug, his embrace feeling like a blanket fresh from the dryer.

Joe let out a sigh. "You're going to do this whether I want you to or not, aren't you?"

"Yes," her soft voice didn't hesitate.

"Okay. Marriage is about compromise, right?"

Donna knew a setup when she heard one. Nerves pricked at her skin. "Right."

"I'm glad you agree."

"Let me guess; you want to plan a big hiking trip when Brent and want me to keep Andrea, AKA Bridezilla, at bay?"

His finger moved like a pendulum between them. His smoldering eyes fixated on hers, telling her that she would enjoy whatever he had planned a whole lot more.

Chapter 27

♥

HIS VAST INTELLIGENCE HAD never helped him win over any ladies. Most women liked that Captain America or Thor look — lots of muscle put to good use. Despite working out and his physical adventures, Joe never considered himself of that superhero caliber.

But based on the way Donna's eyes rolled over his physique, he felt superhuman, inflating his ego slightly.

Donna twirled her ponytail around her forefinger, which rested in front of her shoulder, leaving her neck on the opposite side vulnerable. Joe's eyes gravitated to the bare skin. For a moment, he imagined himself as a vampire. Wasn't there a popular romance series about vampires? He didn't know, but sinking his teeth, playfully, of course, into Donna's neck filled his mind.

His heart slammed against his ribs as he strode toward her. His chest opened wide, and his upper body swayed. The closer he got, the more he noticed the sweet pulse point on Donna's neck throbbing, causing a fire in his lower belly.

His fingers gripped her hips, trying to combat his urge to devour her lips. His feet dragged closer to her, one on either side of hers. Their bodies pressed together. Being this close sent zingers through his legs, stronger than the scorpion attack he'd endured while hiking in the desert last summer.

To him, she was the sun, and the new blooming flowers smiled at her, thanking her simply for being present. Taking his eyes off her seemed impossible, like another body system trying to hijack the nervous system, taking over his brain function. Not. Possible.

"Joe," Donna's tender tone jolted him back from his intense thoughts. Her quick, shallow breathing matched his — he was convinced she wanted this just as badly as he did. Their hot breath mingled as he leaned in and tucked a loose tendril behind her ear.

A quiet gasp escaped Donna when his low, husky voice, already near breathlessness, declared, "Donna, I've never wanted someone as much as I do right now."

His eyes dropped from her full, temping lips to her throat as she swallowed. He feather-tipped his fingers up her bare arms, letting the pad of his thumb caress that exact spot up to her lips. His hands tugged her tight again, eliminating all space between them.

Donna's soft, slender hands gripped his forearms. He loved the feel of this woman's hands on him.

Just barely above a whisper, Donna choked out, "Kiss me, Joe . . . please."

Oh, dear God, her plea at the end did him in. His lips met hers. He unleashed months' worth of want and desire. He wrapped his arm around her lower back, keeping her firmly in place, while his other hand glided up the side of her body, cupping her cheek briefly. Then he cradled the back of her neck, gently tilting her head to the side, deepening the kiss.

A moan erupted from the back of her throat, pushing him further. Something akin to a growl, something he'd never heard from himself before, escaped as he led Donna to the nearest wall, not allowing a millimeter of space between their bodies. Her tight grip on his shoulders felt like heaven. She may have sunk her nails into him, trying to keep her balance. He wouldn't know until later.

He couldn't believe he'd questioned Donna's interest in him. If this kiss were any indicator, she loved him more than anything. Her soft hands ran through his hair as he trailed kisses down her jawline, stopping at that pulse point and thumping erratically.

"Donna," His breathless words whispered in her ear. He felt her shiver under his touch, making his blood run even hotter for his woman. "I need you to tell me to stop."

"Joe," Her tone was serious, grabbing his attention. Her soft hands cupped either side of his face. Chests heaving, they gazed into each other's eyes. No one had ever looked at him like that before. he saw respect and admiration.

Sadness and relief washed over him. She was going to tell him to stop. He didn't want to, but he had to. "You need to stop," her palms dropped from his face and roamed over and down his pecs, where she gripped the sides of his shirt, "after you kiss me like that again."

After a slower, tender kiss, he pressed his forehead against hers and snickered. "We have guests waiting for our direction."

"I need to do this, Joe."

"I know."

"You do?"

Yeah. I don't like it, but I get it. Let's figure out what this entails."

Trailing his hands down her arms, he linked their fingers. They melded perfectly together. Placing one more lingering, sweet kiss on her lips, he asked, "Just one more kiss?" Her smile was enough confirmation for him, knowing this could never be their last kiss.

Donna's head swirled with delight. Her swollen lips molded with Joe's like they were meant to be together. The sharp pokes from his beard scraped against her smooth skin. When they first met, Joe had a smooth face, which she didn't mind. He'd only started growing a beard after she commented that a bit of facial hair was sexy on the right guy. She found that interesting.

He was definitely the *perfect* guy for her. His smooth lips trailed kisses down over her jawline, healing any scrapes she endured. Wrapping her fingers in the grooves of his shoulders revealed his strong muscles. She dwarfed Joe, but the pressure of being sandwiched between the wall and his hard body felt heavenly. She'd never felt more protected in her life.

Oh, wait. He'd told me to make sure he stopped. She'd done the exact opposite but wasn't regretting it. For months, he'd kissed her forehead, cheek, and hand. She'd yearned to feel his lips on her like now. He tasted like traditional pink bubble gum. She found a stash of it in his truck one time. He only chewed it while hiking, until now, apparently.

As great as he tasted, his scent put her over the edge. While he kissed her neck and collarbone, she inhaled his woodsy scent and sighed strongly. "Okay, we need to stop," she declared breathless.

Her palms gently pushed his chest away as her phone rang. "Will you go back to the detectives while I get this?"

Joe kissed her cheek and winked as he retreated toward the living room.

"Hello."

"Hi, Ms. Greer. This is Darcy Littleton. I'm just checking in with you regarding the position."

Silence. Donna wasn't sure what to say. Fortunately, the woman continued.

"After speaking with your employer, I feared you might rescind your acceptance."

"Why?"

"Joe was the man I spoke with. He said you were the most valuable employee he had. Without you, he worried, they would backslide. In addition to your accounting skills, you clearly have great marketing skills."

Donna's eyes stared at the door Joe, her husband, had just walked through. Could she be so selfish? Mom didn't want to go, she'd gotten married. She loved this man. She loved Joe because of his adventure and his carefree, lovable personality. If he moved away, would he still be the same way? Did she want to change that?

"That's interesting. I never knew I meant that much to his company."

"I wondered," Ms. Littleton replied. I'd appreciate it if you wouldn't mind taking twenty-four hours to think about it and get back to me. The reverie in his voice sounded more like a protective, loving boyfriend than an employer — no judgment. I want you on my team, but for the long term, if you get what I'm saying," her words rushed out.

Hearing the things Joe had said made her heart skip a beat. After that kissing — let's be real — make-out session, she needed answers, and Ms. Littleton deserved a committed employee.

"Thank you. I appreciate your insight and flexibility. I'll call you back by tomorrow at this time. Have a wonderful evening, bye."

Tapping the red button and sliding her phone back into her pocket, Donna's eyes roamed over the handsome man pacing in her mom's living room, barely noticing that the detectives were missing.

"Have you had any interesting conversations lately with any women from Texas?"

Joe stopped and slowly turned on his heels. "That's a very specific question."

"I'd like a *very specific* answer."

In two strides, he was within arm's reach. "Did I cost you the job? I wasn't trying to, I promise. She asked questions, and I answered them honestly."

"Hmmm." She nodded slowly.

"Say something, Donna." Joe grabbed her hands and shook them a little, like he was trying to shake her from a daze, if she had been in one, but she wasn't. Her brain was fully aware of everything around her, especially the man in front of her.

"Did you truly mean that you'd be lost without me? Your company will suffer the minute I leave?"

He looked slightly abashed. "She quoted me nicely." Joe took another step closer. Roughness from his beard pressed on her cheek as he leaned closer. With a low, husky tone, he whispered, "I meant every word.

Tears welt up and threatened to cascade down her cheeks. She willed her lip not to quiver. Trembling legs threatened to collapse. Would this be the one time a man didn't abandon her, didn't trade her in for something better?

Emotions overwhelmed her. Grabbing the sides of his already untucked shirt, her doing from the most fantastic make-out session ever, She pulled his torso toward her as she rested her forehead on his chest. "Joe, this is crazy, isn't it?"

His silence caused her heart rate to increase, and her muscles tightened. Why wasn't he answering her?

Ah, Thank you, Lord, for this man. Is he a gift, or are you going to take him from me? Strong arms wrapped her in a cocoon. "What, sweetheart?"

"Sweetheart?" She lifted her head slightly. "Why do you call me that?"

"Would you prefer something different?"

She chuckled. "No, I mean a man only calls a woman sweetheart if he's mocking her or if he cares about her. The tone you use says the latter, but there's so much going on — I feel guilty about not telling our friends about fake dating, your mom left your dad, he's in trouble with his company, my mom's dying because of some crazy man, we got married and I just had the best kiss—er kisses of my life. Then there are activities married couples partake in that we haven't even discussed." She let out a massive sigh, trying to gain her breath back. "I'm truly overwhelmed."

She pulled back and smacked him on the arm for smirking. "Ouch." She knew he was joking. "What was that for?"

"You're teasing me."

"I couldn't help it. You're adorable with your bright pink cheeks, talking about things I've been thinking about for a while."

Holy Moly! The heat in her neck and cheeks rose exponentially. She wrapped her fingers around her neck, trying to hide what was probably beet red by now.

"I promise I won't pressure you to do anything you don't want to do," Joe said, capturing her eyes and speaking with the most sincere, serious eyes she'd ever seen.

She believed him. Joe had been nothing but a gentleman. His cuteness factor exploded at that moment. She'd never tell him that so he could keep his tough, manly image. It was possible for a man as great as Joe to be cute, tough, and sexy.

"Aren't you worried about me pressuring you?" She deadpanned.

His jaw went slack, causing her to giggle. He pulled her back. "Nope. Not worried about that at all."

She huffed a breath before stepping back, pointing at the empty sofa. "Where'd the detectives go?"

"They had to leave. Let's sit, and I'll tell you the plan."

Chapter 28

"R ELAX, DONNA, YOU'RE STANDING out like a sore thumb." Detective Hernandez filled her earpiece.

"I look ridiculous in this wig and glasses."

"The disguise is doing its job. They won't recognize you."

Joe piped up, "For the record, I was going to ask if we could take it home after this was all done with." Laughter from all parties rang through her head.

Once Donna agreed to this plan, things moved quickly. Detective Garcia used an FBI connection in Texas to make sure these men wouldn't get away with their sinister plan.

Undercover police officers surrounded the perimeter of a resort in Belize, where Dr. Campbell and his associates had been tracked down. Joe was in the lobby, accompanied by one of the officers, as it was the stipulation he demanded for Donna to participate in this operation.

Why had she agreed to this? Joe was right; these people—er murderers — were dangerous. If she didn't convince them that she was a doctor, hence giving them access to more victims, they could eliminate her just for their inconvenience.

Donna couldn't help but think of her mom, the reason she was risking her life. Emily and Andrea were at the cancer center in Texas. They were running tests, trying to determine the best treatment for Emily. Hopefully, by the time they arrived at the center, a plan for healing her mom would be well underway.

FBI agents in Texas had already set up a doctor's office — hers — and were waiting for them to return so they could make some arrests.

Wiping her palms down the front of her pantsuit, she took a deep breath and slowly let it out.

"Don't look now, but Dr. Campbell is approaching the bar on your left."

Detective Garcia, tending bar, dipped his chin toward Donna. She peeked over, and shock shot through her body. "Not the same man," Donna's panic ringing in her ear.

"Stay in character," someone spoke into her ear.

"Hey Doc, you ready for another?" Detective Garcia asked, moving closer to calm her down.

"Definitely, thank you." Out of her peripheral vision, she saw the man they'd thought was Dr. Campbell. His eyes sparkled at the announcement of her fake doctor's title.

Taking a dainty sip of her club soda, she returned her attention to her appointment book. Detective Hernandez had argued that this operation spread wide. They'd found evidence that these men were responsible for taking advantage of people who had escaped a terminal diagnosis or were in remission, finding these people in small clinics in Texas and Mexico.

Once spotted in Mexico, they'd moved on to Central America, where they would now be captured, God willing.

Detective Garcia moved to the center of the bar, preoccupying himself with fake activities, such as washing out blenders and spreading the ice throughout the freezer while eavesdropping.

"You're a doctor?"

Donna's head popped up in the man's direction. She tried not to call him a doctor, knowing that no self-respecting doctor would kill their patients for money. She believed these men were posing as doctors, but the ring leader was probably a doctor or had been in the past.

"Yup."

"What kind of doctor?" The man moved two stools closer. Now, only one empty stool separated Donna from the man she'd loved to strangle. It took every ounce of strength for her to stay on script.

"Family practice in Del Rio. I needed a break for a couple of days."

After sipping his bourbon, he set his glass down slowly, spinning the half-full glass. "I know what you mean. Doctoring is tough work."

"Ah, are you a doctor, too?" Donna clasped her trembling hands together and continued to study her faux appointment book, hoping no one noticed. "What field?"

"Internal medicine."

"Nice to meet you," Donna dragged out her last word, waiting for him to provide his name.

"Dr. Campbell."

"What specialty?" Donna briefly glanced at the scumbag next to her. There was a lot worse she could have called him but refrained.

"Hospice and palliative care. Every couple of months, I take a vacation. Dealing with death as much as I do, it's exhausting."

Donna nodded in agreement. "I can imagine." I have a patient right now who's dying. She has a son, but he hasn't come to see her, so she's dying alone, and it breaks my heart."

The stone expression on the man's face alarmed her. Just as she was about to say more, Detective Hernandez spoke into her ear.

"We believe Dr. Campbell is Eli Martinez. His mom died of cancer five years ago. He went on record to say that she was healthy one day, and the next, she had cancer. Once she died, he hunted down the real Dr. Campbell and brutally murdered him, then took his identity and began injecting healthy people with extreme amounts of nitrosamines — cancer-causing chemicals found in some prescription drugs. He has to work with a scientist or someone with a lot of lab knowledge. In a twisted way, I think this is about avenging his mother's death."

"Consider him dangerous. Stay on script," Donna ignored the directive, blaring into her ear.

"Can you imagine that my patient's son had said he was too busy to visit?" Donna shook his head.

"What if he couldn't?"

"Excuse me? What could be more important than visiting your mother on her deathbed?"

The man's steeled response felt like a clutter of spiders crawling on her skin. "Maybe he was figuring out how to make people pay for her death."

Telling her bile in her stomach to stay down, Donna scoffed, "Yeah, that's another major issue. Healthcare has become so outrageously expensive that most refuse treatment. Knowing perfectly well that money wasn't what he meant, she prayed he'd leave it at that.

She worked to get back on the script. "I'm not sure where you're located, but in Del Rio, our hospice workers are overworked and underpaid, leaving us in a precarious position to turn patients away, or by the time services are available, they're no longer needed."

"Nice segway, Donna," Detective Hernandez encouraged through the earpiece.

"I operate with Doctors without Borders, so here's my card." The man reached into his breast pocket and handed her a card. "If you need assistance, call me, and I'll see what I can do." The man took the last shot of his bourbon and slapped the glass on the bar as he slid off the stool.

"Perfect, let him go, Donna," Hernandez's voice vibrated through her head.

"It was nice to meet you. I don't think I caught your name," he prompted, extending his hand.

Nonchalantly, Donna offered her hand. "Dr. Whitney."

The man started to walk away, then turned back with his forefinger in the air. Donna saw Detective Garcia's shoulders tense. "Do you have a business card for me or a website?

Thankfully, Detective Hernadez had done his prep work.

"Of course. Here," Donna held the small card between her forefinger and middle finger.

He inspected the details as if they would tell him where to find the lost covenant. "I'll be in touch," he said.

Donna watched the man walk away. She turned back into the bar, gaining Detective Garcia's attention. She could tell by the nervous look in his eyes he thought something was amiss.

Chapter 29

❤

"OH, MOM, THAT'S great to hear." Donna gripped the phone tighter. "Give Andrea my best. I'm settled and waiting; don't worry. The entire office is bugged with sound and video. I'm watching the agents in the waiting room pretending to read magazines; it's entertaining. I wonder how many rooms we've been in before, and agents were fitting into the environment without us knowing; they are so good at what they do."

"Focus, Donna. You know what to say, right?" Her mom asked.

"Yes, You just work on getting better, Mom."

"Take care, baby."

Donna disconnected the call as he heard Dr. Campbell announce his arrival to the secretary, Millie, a Senior Field Agent. From her hidden screen, Donna spied two goons with the fake doctor. The taller one reminded her of Tony Soprano.

Joe's voice came through her earpiece. "This could get interesting."

"Just relax. Remember, this is our day job," Detective Garcia quipped.

"As long as you keep Donna safe, I won't complain."

Five agents posed as patients in the waiting room; two agents were in Donna's office, waiting in the closet, ready to reveal themselves, when Donna either said the safe word or they moved in to arrest the men.

"Please take a seat, and I'll let Dr. Whitney know you're here."

She couldn't help but focus her attention on Joe. Even through a screen, he was the most handsome man she'd ever met. Joe ran his hand down his face. Donna had seen him do this when he was nervous or flustered. They never had the opportunity to talk the other night, but as soon as the FBI arrested these murderers, she would tell Joe how she felt.

She waited for the Detective Hernandez's direction. Everything about this situation reeked of trouble. She'd never admit it to Joe, but maybe she shouldn't have agreed to this sting operation.

"Note the shorter one has a gun on his hip," one of the agents in the waiting room whispered into her ear.

"Dr. Whitney will be out for you shortly," Millie informed. the men.

Before leaving her office, she spoke aloud for everyone to hear. "This is not the man from my mother's house. Where is he?"

"Patience is a significant part of his job, Donna. If I had to guess, the man who came to your mother's house is a new recruit or someone lower on the totem pole per sé This man who calls himself Dr. Campbell is probably the leader or close to the leader. Follow the script, and you'll be fine," Detective Hernandez had the patience of Job. Hopefully, he had God's protection like Job did.

"Lord, please help us get closer to solving this case, calm my nerves, give me the words I need to say, and get us home safely to our families. Amen."

A chorus of 'Amen' filled her ear, bringing a smile to her face.

Less than five minutes later, Donna appeared in the waiting room. "Hello, Dr. Campbell; it's good to see you again," Donna said, extending her hand. "You brought friends?"

A sinister chuckle escaped the doctor's mouth. "I never go anywhere without them."

"Yet, this is the first time I'm meeting them. That's interesting." Donna waved her hand for them to follow. "Come on back, gentleman."

"I must say I'm surprised that you contacted me, Dr. Campbell. What can I do for you?"

"It's not what you can do for me, but what I can do for your patients."

"I'm sorry I don't follow you," her eyes darted among the men.

"You said there are a lot of folks who need hospice. We can partner together for the sake of these people's health."

Donna crossed her legs at the ankle, hoping to prevent them from seeing her trembling muscles. She repeated the process with her hands, setting her clasped fingers on her desk. She leaned forward slightly.

"Tell me what you're thinking."

Listening to Dr. Campbell explain how he could provide her with ten hospice nurses in the name of helping good people be comfortable almost made her lose her composure. She knew her defenses were down. Feeling vulnerable, Donna banged out a breath as she asked, "Are you claiming that you can heal these people?"

"Donna, stay on script," Detective Garcia growled in her ear.

Ominous laughter filled the room. Dr. Campbell's intense observation of her face spiked her jitters. "Sweet Dr. Whitney, you know people in hospice are nearing the end. The reality is they will pass on to the other world sooner rather than later, and it's my job to make them comfortable."

The big buffoons with the evil Eli Martinez, posing as a doctor, had the nerve to laugh. She needed to get out of this room immediately, but what if she left and they started snooping? She'd put the hidden agents in danger.

"Give me a moment, gentlemen," she used that term loosely. "Millie, what does our hospice list look like?"

"That sounds great. Can I have that address, please?" Donna neatly printed the address to a house used by FBI agents. I'll need the code, too."

"You got this," Millie said before she hung up, giving Donna the strength she needed to finish this meeting.

Once they left, she could check on her mom. Plastering a smile on her face, she handed over the meticulously well-written address and gate code for her patient.

"Doris Everhart. How old is she?"

That wasn't in the script. Donna's heart started to race. "Let me check." She tapped on the keyboard, giving herself time to guess how old Agent Frost looked since she'd be the one posing as Doris. "She not very old at all. Fallen victim to cancer at the ripe old age of forty."

"Thanks, Donna, I'm actually forty-five," the agent chuckled through the earpiece. Donna wished she could see the agents arrest these men. *Sorry, Lord, I know that's not what I should think.*

"I can assure you, your patient is in the best hands possible."

Donna cringed as a leery smile spread across the man's face. She steeled her spine before she responded. "I'm counting on it."

"Who are you? What happened to the sweet, *I don't want to ruffle anyone's feathers,* woman I married?"

Donna clutched her trembling hands. "Getting justice for my mom is important." She shrugged her shoulders. "Putting these men away before they can hurt anyone else is equally important."

Joe grabbed Donna's wrist and tugged her to his chest. He kissed tenderly on the inside of her wrist, and she shuttered. "I'm so proud of you."

"I want to take my wife out to celebrate. If you don't mind me saying, you are one hot doctor." He pulled on the lab coat she wore in the set-up.

She playfully slapped him on the shoulder. "Don't be silly," she giggled like a teenage girl.

"I'm not," Joe said, leaning in.

Donna couldn't wait to leave and talk to Joe. They'd spend the first part of the evening sharing their feelings, and then they'd work on perfecting their kissing in the second half. "Let's go—"

Detective Hernandez shoved the closet door open, cutting her sentence off. "—That was great, Donna. By tomorrow night, Dr Campbell, AKA Eli Martinez, will be in custody."

"How are you going to get the men they work for? He has to have someone get him the medicine. The detectives shared a copious look with the agents who'd entered just a beat before. Donna knew that look. She wanted to know the rest of the plan, but the FBI worked a lot like the military—you knew what they wanted you to know and nothing more.

"Thanks for keeping my woman alive," Joe said, stepping back from Donna and shaking the detectives' hands.

"She kept herself alive—"

"—and the rest of us," One of the female agents interrupted.

"The agents in the parking lot followed the men to a house downtown, so you are free to leave. We'll contact you if we need anything further, but this should be an open and shut case." Detective Garcia shook both Donna and Joe's hands.

Donna watched Joe swallow his disappointment as she shed the doctor's coat and handed it to the agent. "Good luck to all of you. Stay safe."

Peace washed over Donna as Joe led her to the car. She wasn't sure of the effects her mom would face, but Donna hoped it wasn't too late to save her mom.

Chapter 30

♥

TIPPING HIS HEAD BACK against the couch in the hotel room, Joe's mind whirled. "Mom, you can't avoid this forever. If you divorce him, it might be ugly, but you don't know that. The papers are tearing him down to size; this could be in your favor.

"Joseph Hartley, that is not the way I raised you. Thinking of self-gain while your dad is struggling."

"A problem he brought on himself," he muttered.

"Maybe so, but that's still no reason to desert someone. What would Jesus do?"

Frustration flowed through his veins. "I get it, Mom, but Jesus is perfect; I am not. I have hard feelings on top of the anger and disgust for the way he's treated me."

"And it's only hurting you. Like you said, your dad is dealing with his image. He is determined to throw one of his engineers under the bus—"

"—Exactly! He wanted it to be me. Someone he could bully and overpower. I hope those engineers have the courage to speak the truth, just like Jesus would. He knew he was throwing her own words back at her, but his mom had defended Ivan Hartley one too many times."

Beverly let out a long breath. "Joe, if he agrees to get help, I will be there for him."

Joe's heart jarred. He simply wanted his parents to be happy, particularly his mom, who deserved someone to shower her with affection. "I don't doubt it. You are loving and loyal." Joe bit his lip, hoping it would prevent him from saying anything to hurt his mom. She was right in her thinking and only trying to help, but this was a difficult situation.

"How's Emily doing?" Beverly changed the subject.

Joe suspected this conversation would come up. "We're not sure. Yesterday, Donna spoke to her on the phone, and she said she felt great. Today, she's barely responsive. Andrea called Donna about ten minutes ago. I'm waiting for Donna to get out of the shower so I can tell her."

"Poor Donna. Anything come of the case?"

Joe ran his fingers through his hair. "We're not getting updates from the FBI, nor are the detectives contacting us. I assume everything went down the way it was supposed to, or we would have heard about it on the news, right?"

"I imagine. I didn't spend much time with Emily, but she is someone I would enjoy getting to know better. I hope she makes it through this okay. She's in the best treatment center in the nation, so I'm sending prayers for answers and healing."

"Thanks, Mom. She is a great woman. I need to thank Emily for pushing me to marry Donna so she could be part of it—"

Joe froze his pacing and squeezed his eyes shut at the sound of a woman clearing her throat. He caught the look in Donna's eyes as he turned to face her. Pain, but a lot of anger resided within her. "Mom, we'll talk later. Bye."

A pang jolted through her body. Red filled her vision. *Are those floating stars?* "I was such a fool. How could you, Joe?" She didn't let him respond before she continued her tirade. "Was the pastor real, or was this a fake marriage? What, fake dating wasn't bad enough? Everyone must think I am the world's biggest idiot."

Joe stepped closer but stopped when Donna put her palms up, forcing him to stop.

He acknowledged her request with a nod and stepped back. "No one thinks you're stupid. Your mom said she saw our love for each other and wanted to see her *baby girl walk down the aisle.* I just expedited things so she could."

"I told you I wanted to get married once and only once." Her chin dipped, and she sank onto the bed. "I wanted to be loved."

"I do love you," Joe blurted out, rushing to the side of the bed. On his knees in front of her, he tucked a piece of hair behind her ear and wiped the tears that had started to fall. "Don't cry. Nothing changes. My true feelings are complete and utter love for you. I wanted to make sure your mom was happy, too."

"Perfect." Spiciness dripped from her tone. "I'm glad you made sure my mom's feelings were at the top of the list for *our* wedding. Who came up with such a stupid idea anyway?"

Sheepishly, Joe whispered, "Your mom. Turns out convenient marriages are a big hit in romance novels."

"What?! You created our lives based on a romance novel. Of all the stupid, idiotic—"

"—I'm confused. I thought women wanted their spouse to act like the guys in romance novels." Joe interrupted her. She'd never admit it, but she was glad he'd prevented her from saying anything worse.

Donna hesitated, opened her mouth to speak, and closed it again. Joe's argument had some merit. She had never conducted formal research, but she suspected that women often turned to romance novels as an escape. Perhaps her mother had done the same, living vicariously through the characters' love stories on the page. For many readers, the fictional world probably offered a welcome respite from the disappointments of their own love lives.

Over the past few months, her life had seemed like a romance novel. She'd felt giddy like a teenager, and Joe had given her so many swoon-worthy moments she relished daily.

"You might have a valid point, but I'm so angry that I'm not thinking straight."

Joe sat back on his heels. "Look, Donna. I am madly in love with you." He wiped his palm over his face. I planned on telling you about this the other night, but other things happened..." Donna recalled the kiss the other night and felt her cheeks flush.

"Yeah, I'd planned on telling you that I was in love with you and was so happy that we got married; I guess it's a good thing neither of us had the opportunity to say anything. At least we got in a great kiss before the truth of this rogue marriage tore us apart."

"What?!" Joe's expression of shock hit Donna hard. The muscles in his jaw twitched, but whether he was angry or not didn't matter to her. He had lied to her, and she couldn't believe that anyone would marry someone under false pretenses. She should have trusted her instincts; she had known all along that he was up to something.

"I'm going to visit my mom and Andrea—"

"—Yeah, Andrea called while you were in the shower. Your mom is having a rough day, so we should get there quickly. We'll talk about this later."

Donna's head throbbed. How much more could she take? In her mind, she was already past her limit, but clearly, the Lord thought she had emotional strength compared to Thor's muscles. Not likely.

A staring contest ensued. Donna blew out an exasperated breath. "I'm going to the treatment center. I think it's best you head home. Brent needs you."

"You're kidding?" Still on his knees, Joe rested his hands on the upper part of his quads.

"I need time to think, and I can't do that with you here."

He leaned forward, resting his hand on her knee. "If that's what you want, I'll do it, but not before I tell you a few things."

"I won't stop you." The boyish grin that pulled at his lips seared her heart.

"From the moment I met you," he sucked in a breath, "you left me dumbfounded." He sat at an angle on the bed, holding her hand. Her heart raced as he drew small circles over her knuckles. "When you came back that night, I knew I had to have you, but with my track record, I didn't think you'd give me a chance."

"So you came up with the fake dating plan?"

"I thought I'd learned what happiness was that day, but I was wrong."

Given his smirk, Donna wondered what unattractive look tarried on her face.

"My heart almost broke with joy the day you said you'd marry me."

Even if she tried, Donna couldn't stop the tears. For years, Donna had covered up her hurt by avoiding or smiling, but now Joe had ripped those coping mechanisms out of her system, and she sat vulnerable in front of him.

"I love you, Donna. Whether we married when we did or waited until later, I couldn't love you any more than I do right now. Technically, I'm going to head home, but I'm not going anywhere in the sense of us. I'll be at home waiting for you to return. Take the time you need to wrap your head around this because when you get home, I'm not letting you go."

His words were hypnotic, and Donna felt numb. Everywhere. If he had said these things earlier, there would have been no question, but now, hearing them after the fact stung a lot. Nonetheless, she couldn't deny that the boulders she'd placed in a neat circle around her heart were starting to shift.

She finally blinked. "Thank you for understanding. I'm going to see my mom now," Donna felt like a robot set to automatic. Attempting to stand, Joe tugged her back down.

"Just one more thing." Joe weaved his fingers through her hair and crushed his lips to hers. He grunted when she parted her lips, instantly allowing him to deepen the kiss. He eliminated all space between them as his hands roamed along her upper and lower back. He slowed the kiss down, allowing himself to examine as many aspects of his wife as possible.

When Donna slid her arms over his chest and around his neck, she ran her fingers through his hair, massaging the scalp. He murmured a moan against her mouth, which she returned. Her heavenly sound was more than he could handle. Blood rushed like a waterslide through his nervous system, sending intense urges throughout his entire body. *If only Donna were ready for every facet of marriage.*

Briefly catching his breath, he trailed kisses down her jaw. She tilted her head, giving him better access to her neck. Having Donna in his arms gave him that same freefall thrill as skydiving. His mouth returned to hers with a passion that hopefully said, 'I love you' and 'I'll always protect you.'

Donna was the first to pull away. "Wow. I think we'll have to stay married. You've ruined me for every other man on the face of the Earth. Where'd you learn to kiss like that?" She shook her head. "Never mind, I don't want to know."

"You already know my story, so that was all God bringing us together." His hands lingered on her hips, and a slow grin spread across his face. "Hopefully, that kiss will remind you of what's waiting for you. If not, at least it will give me something to dream about for the rest of my life. I'm packing up and heading to the airport. Please keep me in the loop on how your mom is doing."

A keen awareness sparked her system. She didn't need to run anymore. "We'll talk soon," Donna's sweet voice filled his ears before she let the hotel room door slam shut.

I will do everything I can to keep my wife!

Chapter 31

♥

O N HER WAY TO the center, Donna received a call from Detective Hernandez. "Donna, I just wanted to let you know that because of your work, we got the three you helped us step up and the scientist mastermind behind the entire operation."

"That is great to hear."

"It wouldn't have happened without you and Joe. These men were hurt and taking it out on innocent people."

"Everyone on your end safe and sound?"

"No one on our side was injured during the takedown," the detective chuckled. How's your mom?"

"It's not looking good, but God's in charge."

"Donna, I understand this is a difficult time for you. Rest assured, these criminals will face severe consequences for their actions. They will serve multiple life sentences, holding them accountable for every life they took."

"I will. Thank you for all you did." She disconnected the call as she pulled into the parking lot.

Once Donna thanked Andrea for staying with her mom, she called her friend an Uber, convincing her to get home to Brent. Donna crawled into her mother's hospital bed with her. The agony her heart faced overwhelmed her. She did the only thing she could think of — pray.

Lord, I don't have any easy decisions, but you already know that. What are you trying to show me? Please give me peace that passes understanding. I'd also like clear answers.

Donna chuckled, knowing that God wasn't her lackey and that He'd do whatever He wanted, when and how He wanted. She just hoped she didn't miss the opportunities. Her eyelids, heavier than her heart, gently closed.

Unaware of how long she'd been asleep, her eyes jarred open at the sound of her ringtone. "Hello."

"How have you been?" Joe's voice, stiff and raspy, broke into her thoughts. She felt the vibration from his deep voice in her low belly. *Take me now, Jesus. It would be less painful.*

"Mom's still sleeping. Doctors believe the drugs those monsters injected into her are shutting down her nervous system and, ultimately, her brain will stop working." Donna sniffed.

"Sweetheart, I am so sorry. If only I were there to hold you."

She thought the same thing at the exact moment. "Yeah."

"I've got some news. I'm unsure if it's good or bad, but Mom returned to the house to support Dad in his legal troubles. Tomorrow, he's making things right, financially speaking. He's awarding the families affected by his company's negligence a pretty penny."

Donna sighed and moved from her mother's bed to the adjacent chair. "How are you feeling?"

"I'm not sure. I hope Dad has learned his lesson, but he's thrown money at people before, and yet here he is again, so I'm less convinced this time around."

Wiping her eyes, she saw the clock on the hospital wall. "Joe, it's four o'clock in the morning for you. Have you slept?"

His sweet chuckle filled Donna with joy. She didn't even wait for his answer before she blurted, "I am deeply, madly in love with you, Joseph Hartley. I can't think of anything else."

"I—"

"Please, let me finish Joe before I chicken out again." When he didn't say anything, she continued. "The rejection in my life caused me to avoid anything and anyone that might reject me. The fake dating was perfect because I spent time with the funniest, sexiest, most caring man on God's green Earth. As much as I told my heart not to get involved, it didn't listen. You had my heart from the moment you saved me from a concussion after I zip-lined the first time. I never expected your dating suggestion; I just wanted more time with you. Since Andrea clearly liked Brent, I gave it a try, hoping to protect myself if, or rather when, you rejected me. My actions or reactions have nothing to do with you but rather my insecurity, and I'm sorry if I upset you or made you feel worse. I know you've got your own issues. Okay, I think I'm done."

Silence.

"Joe, are you there?"

"Yeah, give me a minute to pick myself off the floor."

"Stop teasing me. I just poured my heart out to you," a nervous giggle escaped Donna.

"Wow," there was more silence. "Where to start? I love you so much. I fell in love with you before we even left for Hawaii, and Satan pumped me full of doubt like a body-builder pumps steroids." A laugh burst from her, but she reined in her shock so he'd continue. "I was testing the waters in Hawaii. I had a great speech that I'd planned, and instead, the word dissolve, which starting right now is no longer in either of our vocabulary, came out instead. I was so afraid that you didn't feel anything and wouldn't open to seeing if you could have feelings for me that I pushed you away, in words anyway. When your mom told me she could see that you loved me, I felt like Thor when no one could lift his hammer — you were all mine, and I won't lie; I puff my chest out a little more at the thought. I'm so sorry I hurt you."

Tears stained her cheeks. Through her sniffles, she declared, "I wish you were here."

"You want more kisses, aye?"

"No, well, yes, that was amazing, but just being in your strong arms would be perfect right now."

Donna heard rustling through the phone. "What are you doing?"

"Walking. It helps clear my head but also gets me closer to the one I love."

"Joe!" Donna shrieked, jumping out of her chair. She ran to her husband, who stood in her mother's treatment room doorway. "I thought you left."

He wrapped his arms around her, tugging her against his chest; he kissed her forehead and squeezed her tight. "That was the plan, but when you left to come here, I broke down," his palms grabbed her shoulders, guiding her away from his body; he met her eyes, "Don't you dare tell anyone,"

She smirked, using her finger to trace a cross over her heart, she promised, "Wife's honor," then rested against his chest again.

"You are everything to me. I promise never to turn you away. If you ever feel like I am doing so, please don't hesitate to tell me. Let's not wait until it becomes a big issue. I married you because I love you deeply, and that love will never fade away."

"I love you, Joseph Hartley."

"I love you too, Mrs. Joseph Hartley," a wide, joy–filled grin filled his face.

Donna's hands drifted along his strong biceps before she wound her arms around his neck. Pressing her lips against his, she felt his love for her. And his acceptance. An ac–ceptance that she'd never experienced before but now felt confident it would always be there. God had gifted her with this amazing man with whom she couldn't wait to explore the world.

BONUS EPILOGUE

Thank you for reading Joe and Donna's story. I hope you loved Let Me Marry You. Do you want to find out what happened to Emily Greer and Ivan Hartley? Click this link to sign up for my newsletter and read the free bonus epilogue.If you are reading this in paperback format, head to trueheartromance.com for the bonus epilogue link.

How About a Review?

YOUR FEEDBACK IS VALUABLE, so please consider sharing your thoughts. This will help other readers discover this book and my other works.

Thank you from the bottom of my heart for reading and reviewing my book(s).

Amazon

Goodreads

Bookbub

Acknowledgements

"And whatever you do, whether in word or deed, do it all in the name of the Lord Jesus, giving thanks to God the Father through him." ~ Colossians 3:17

This book would not have been possible without The Good Lord's support and encouragement. It may be cliché, but I believe it wholeheartedly!

I had the time of my life working with my daughter on this project. She wrote the couple's wedding song. The brainstorming, her guitar and piano playing, and finally, her beautiful singing made me smile. She has a real talent that I hope she pursues.

I appreciate my editor, Ann LaCombe, and all her wisdom. Her keen eye is a skill I admire and revere. Thank you for making my writing even better.

To all my readers — you are invaluable! Thank you for your support. With all the possibilities you have, you read *Let Me Marry You.* It's an honor that you chose one of my books to read, without you, I wouldn't be an author. Thank you for bringing me along into your life. Until we meet again...

About the Author

Karen Tucci, a public school teacher by profession, now tutors writing students online and homeschools her two children.

A native of Maine, she has trekked miles of the Pine Tree State and visited countless others. It is through her life experiences that the basis for her romance stories develop. One of her favorite things to say when out adventuring is, "...that is definitely going in my next book!"

Fun fact: Karen had only read and wrote non-fiction growing up. It wasn't until her late twenties that she embraced the joy brought forth by doing both — reading and writing — within the different romance tropes. Now she reads at least fifteen fiction novels a month and writes daily!

Connect with Karen:

<u>Facebook Reader's Group.</u>
To find out about special deals, giveaways, and new releases, join her newsletter:
<u>https://www.trueheartromance.com</u>
<u>Instagram</u>
<u>Goodreads</u>
<u>Bookbub</u>
<u>Amazon</u>